KT-102-910

DISNEY'S
FAMILY
Treasury

To Ally
with love
from Marina
x

Adapted by Sheryl Kahn, Ann Braybrooks, Vanessa Elder
and Rita Walsh-Balducci

Contents

Stories About Family

Stories About Honesty and Integrity

Stories About Love and Friendship

Stories About Courage and Responsibility

Stories About Family

A Whale of a Tale

from *Pinocchio*

To become a real boy, all the wooden puppet, Pinocchio, had to do was be brave, truthful, and unselfish. But he was having trouble living up to any of those ideals. He had already lied to the Blue Fairy. And then he had been weak and selfish by going to Pleasure Island, where he had smoked cigars, played pool, and almost been turned into a donkey.

Ashamed, Pinocchio swam back to the mainland with Jiminy Cricket. Outside Geppetto's workshop, Pinocchio cried, "Father! Father, I'm home!"

No one answered. Geppetto was gone. And, from the look of the dust and cobwebs, he had been gone a while.

As Pinocchio and Jiminy sat outside, a dove dropped a piece of paper at their feet. The note said

that Geppetto had gone looking for Pinocchio and been swallowed by a whale named Monstro. Apparently Geppetto was still alive inside the whale, which was resting at the bottom of the sea.

"I'm going to find my father," Pinocchio declared. "I'm going to the bottom of the sea."

On a high cliff, Pinocchio tied a heavy rock to his tail. Jiminy grabbed hold of the rope and plunged into the water with Pinocchio.

At the bottom of the sea, Jiminy grabbed a smaller rock to use as a weight. Pinocchio wandered into a school of fish, and before he knew it, he was swept into the whale's belly.

Pinocchio saw his father sitting forlornly in his fishing boat. "Father!" cried Pinocchio. "I've come to save you."

"No, Pinocchio. There's no way out. Monstro only opens his mouth when he's eating. Then everything comes in—nothing goes out."

Pinocchio thought hard. "Father! We'll build a big fire, and the smoke will make Monstro sneeze!"

They started a blaze with some of the wood from Geppetto's boat.

As the flames grew, Pinocchio and Geppetto hastily built a raft with the remaining wood.

The whale shook, then sneezed. The tremendous force sent the little raft hurtling out of Monstro's mouth.

The furious whale swam beneath the raft and thrust it into the air. Geppetto and Pinocchio tumbled into the sea. "Hurry, Father!" cried Pinocchio.

"I can't make it, son. Save yourself."

"No, Father, I won't leave you!" Pinocchio grabbed Geppetto's shirt and dragged him to shore. There was no way he was going to lose sight of his father now.

Later, after both Pinocchio and Geppetto
were safely at home, the Blue Fairy rewarded
Pinocchio by making him into a real boy.
He had proven himself brave, truthful,
and *unselfish*.

Trouble Under the Sea

from *The Little Mermaid*

More than anything else, Ariel loved exploring shipwrecks and finding human treasures. But her father, King Triton, had expressly ordered her to stay away from shipwrecks, or any place where she would be in danger of being snagged by one of those fish-eating humans.

The Little Mermaid knew her father loved her. But she also knew that he just didn't understand. Human objects were so amazing, and shipwrecks were the only place she could find them. Nothing would happen to her. She was sure of it.

One day, Ariel took her friend Flounder to see a new shipwreck she had found. "Isn't it fantastic?" she said.

"Yeah, sure," replied Flounder, anxiously looking over his shoulder. "It's great. Now let's get out of here."

"You're not getting cold fins now, are you?" Ariel asked.

"Who, me?" said Flounder. "No way. It's just, uh, it looks damp in there. I think I may be coming down with something." He coughed loudly, making sure that Ariel heard.

"All right," said Ariel. "You can just stay here and watch for sharks."

"What? Sharks! Ariel!" Flounder tried to swim after Ariel through a porthole, but he got stuck. "Ariel, help!"

Ariel grabbed Flounder's fins and pulled him inside the ship. Soon she spied a shiny silver object. She picked it up and said, "Have you ever seen anything so wonderful?"

As they examined the object, Flounder was distracted by a strange sound. "What was that?" he asked, trembling.

"Flounder, will you relax?" said Ariel, picking up and examining another object. "Nothing is going to happen."

Flounder heard the strange sound again. He thought he saw a shadow. Looking behind him, he saw a huge shark was gliding toward them. "Shark! Shark!" he cried.

Flounder zoomed toward a porthole and got stuck again. As the shark bore down on him, its huge jaws open wide, Ariel swam up and pushed Flounder through the porthole. Then she followed, swimming as fast as she could.

The shark raced after them. In Flounder's haste to get away, he smacked into the ship's mast. Dazed, he sank to the ocean floor.

Ariel reached through a metal anchor ring and grabbed her friend. As she backed out of the ring, the shark tried to follow, but it got stuck. The shark thrashed its tail, frustrated at not being able to catch its prey.

Ariel and Flounder swam back to the palace. Ariel thought about how her father had been right. Shipwrecks were dangerous!

Stormy Night

from *The Old Mill*

In an abandoned windmill, a blue barn swallow accepted a worm from her mate. All day, she had been sitting on her nest, keeping her three eggs warm. Together she and her mate had built the nest in a cog hole of an old millstone.

The blue barn swallows were not the only animals who had made the mill their home. Bright-eyed bats clustered in the rafters. A plump old owl perched on a wooden beam. Often the barn swallows watched the owl fluff his feathers and swivel his head from left to right, right to left.

On this night, the barn swallow watched the bats unfold their wings and dart toward a hole in the side of the mill. For a moment, moonlight illuminated their ragged shapes. Then the moon disappeared behind thick clouds, and the bats burst into darkness. Her mate followed them into the night to look for more food.

Inside the mill it was quiet, except for the soft, occasional hooting of the owl. The barn swallow shifted on her nest. As she blinked in the darkness, she felt a cold wind blow through the chinks in the walls. Then the wind shook the mill and howled.

Rain started to fall. The drops fell one at a time, then pounded the roof in a steady rhythm. Water seeped in through holes in the roof, but did not drip onto the nest.

The wind shrieked louder. Suddenly the mother swallow saw the huge mill wheel coming toward her. The wind had snapped the rope that held the mill wheel, and the arms of the old mill had begun to move, turning the wheel inside with them.

In fright, the swallow darted away from her nest. Then she flew back and sheltered the eggs with her wings. The big, heavy wheel rolled over her nest, but the swallow and her eggs escaped being crushed. The cog that matched the hole containing her nest was broken.

All through the night, the swallow remained on her nest to protect her eggs. When the storm died down, the windmill ceased to turn and the sun glowed through the many chinks in the old, abandoned mill. She was glad to see her mate return. He brought food for their newly hatched children.

Cruella's Wicked Puppy Plan

from *101 Dalmatians*

It was a cold, dark night. The snow swirled and the wind blew, but Pongo and Perdita raced across the countryside with only one thought on their minds: They had to save their puppies!

Cruella De Vil had stolen their puppies, and many more besides. She had hidden them in an old house far from London. She planned to make Dalmatian coats out of them!

With a ferocious growl, Pongo leaped into the house where the puppies were kept. Perdita showed the ninety-nine puppies how to escape, while Pongo bravely snapped and jumped at Cruella's dim-witted henchmen. Once the puppies were safely outside, Pongo and Perdita led them away from the De Vil house.

The snow was deep, making it hard for the group to go very fast. Pongo and Perdita knew that Cruella would be after them. To make sure they didn't leave pawprints in the snow, Pongo and Perdita had the puppies follow them on a frozen stream. Soon the headlights from Cruella's car shone in the darkness. The Dalmatian family had to hide under a bridge.

"That was a close one, Perdy," Pongo said.

"I'm c-c-c-cold," Lucky said, shivering.

"And I'm hungry," said Rolly.

Pongo and Perdita brought the puppies to a barn, where they all rested for the night. The cows had never seen so many dogs in one place. They happily shared their milk with the puppies.

In the morning, the dogs were on their way again. Cruella was still looking for them, so they hid in an old blacksmith's shop. Soon the playful puppies were romping around in the ashes.

"That gives me an idea!" Pongo cried. "Come on, everybody, roll in the soot. I want all of you good and dirty!"

Shortly after, one hundred and one black dogs nervously marched across the street, right under Cruella's nose. The plan had worked! The dogs were able to board a truck bound for London, and were soon on their way home.

Roger and Anita were very surprised when they heard Pongo barking at the door.

"Pongo, old boy! Is it really you?" Roger cried when they ran in. The house was quickly filled with happy, dirty, playful puppies.

"But, Roger, what will we do with them all?" Anita asked.

"We'll keep them!" Roger cried. "Families stick together!"

Home, Sweet Home

from *Peter Pan*

T he Darling children had heard many wonderful stories about Peter Pan, but they never dreamed they would ever really meet him. So when Peter Pan flew into the nursery one night, they were delighted.

"Come with me to Never Land," Peter told Wendy, John, and Michael. And so they did, flying through the night sky with him and his pixie friend, Tinker Bell.

Never Land was filled with all sorts of interesting people. The Lost Boys were Peter Pan's friends, and they were very excited that he had brought some new children to play with them.

"This is Wendy," Peter Pan explained. "And I've brought her here to be your mother."

Wendy shook her head. "I can't be their mother," she explained. "I still need my own mother too much."

None of the Lost Boys had mothers of their own anymore. "What's a mother?" one of the Lost Boys asked Wendy.

Wendy felt very sorry for them. "She a wonderful person who loves you very much," Wendy told them.

Peter Pan frowned. The Lost Boys seemed more interested in mothers than in playing pirates.

Wendy went on. "A mother tells you wonderful stories and kisses you good night at the end of the day."

"Are you our mother?" Michael asked Wendy.

"Of course not," Wendy said. "I'm your sister. Don't you remember our real mother?"

John picked up his hat. "I remember her, Wendy!" he cried. "And I propose we go home to her at once!"

Wendy, John, and Michael said good-bye to Peter Pan and his friends. Never Land grew smaller and smaller as they flew through the sky toward home, where their own mother was just getting ready to kiss them all good night.

King Triton's Gift

from *The Little Mermaid*

King Triton was exuberant. Together, he and Eric had defeated the wicked sea witch, Ursula, and saved the merpeople from her evil schemes. But before he could rejoice, he had to find Ariel. He knew that his daughter would not be happy until she was rejoined with her true love.

Triton hadn't approved of Eric, or of any humans for that matter. He had seen too many sea creatures snagged by their cruel fisheaters'

hooks. But now he realized that Eric was different. Eric had risked his own life to save Ariel—and for that, Triton would always be grateful.

Sebastian and Flounder led the Sea King to the shore where Ariel was sitting on a rock. She was mournfully watching Eric as he lay unconscious on the sand.

Triton turned to Sebastian. "She really does love him, doesn't she?"

"Mmm." Sebastian agreed.

"Well then, I guess there's just one problem left," mused the King.

"What's that, Your Majesty?"

"How much I'm going to miss her." Sebastian's jaw fell open. With a sigh, Triton raised his trident and sent a beam of magical light toward Ariel.

As Ariel looked down to see what was happening, she saw her fish tail being transformed into legs—human legs like she had always dreamed! She looked up and beamed at her father.

Eric began to stir. When he saw Ariel walking toward him out of the ocean, his face lit up. At last they were free! And they belonged to each other.

King Triton smiled sadly. He knew that he would not be able to see his remarkable daughter every day as he had in the past. But he was warmed by the knowledge that she would have a happy future with a man who loved her as much as he did.

A Forest in Flames

from *Bambi*

A careless hunter had forgotten to put out his campfire, and now the whole forest was ablaze. Bambi and his father tried to make their way through the burning trees, but as the wind changed direction, so did the fire.

Bambi's father used all his experience with forest fires to find a path through the blazing woods. As Bambi ran for his life, he felt stronger knowing that his wise father was by his side.

They ran through a stream, hoping the water would protect them from the flames. But the trees along the banks were ablaze, too.

At last Bambi and his father came to a waterfall. The trees behind them were burning. Trapped, they had only one choice: to jump.

They landed with a great splash. Exhausted, they swam slowly to an island in the middle of the river.

Nearby, Faline stood at the water's edge, looking up at the hills. She fearfully watched her forest burn. She, too, was weakened by fatigue, but she could not rest until she knew Bambi was safe.

As she listened and watched, she heard splashing. Two stags were walking toward her through the shallow water. As they emerged from the smoky haze, she recognized them.

"Bambi!" she cried.

Though he was very tired and sore, Bambi dashed through the water toward Faline's voice. He climbed up on the rock beside her. She was alive!

The deer stood close together and watched their forest burn. With heavy hearts, they realized that many animals would now lose their homes. They were grateful, though, to be safe and to at least have each other.

A New Home for Tod

from *The Fox and the Hound*

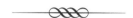

From her nest in the old oak tree, a wise owl called Big Mama witnessed the whole sad event.

She was just settling down for bed when a terrified mother fox burst out of the woods. The fox was carrying a newborn kit in her mouth.

She quickly hid her baby in the tall grass by a fence and then tore across the meadow, clearly running for her life. She was followed closely by a pack of baying hounds.

Moments later, Big Mama heard rifle shots. She knew that the baby fox was now alone in the world.

Big Mama flew down to the baby. "You poor little fella," she crooned, stroking his fur. He was shivering. "You're gonna need some carin' for."

The baby fox snuggled against Big Mama's soft chest.

"Oh, no! Not me, darlin'." Big Mama laughed. "But don't you move. Big Mama's gonna be right back."

She flew off in search of her friends Boomer and Dinky. She found them in a nearby tree, where they were trying to rout a stubborn caterpillar from his hole.

"Boomer!" Big Mama called to the woodpecker. "Stop that peckin' and listen. I need you and Dinky to help me."

She told them about the little fox and his mother.

"Gosh," said Boomer, "who'll take care of him?"

Dinky the sparrow ruffled his feathers.

"Hey! I got an idea!" he exclaimed. "The Widow Tweed is all alone. She'd probably be happy to take care of him. And I'll tell ya how we'll arrange it . . ."

A few minutes later, the plan was set. Boomer tapped on the door of Widow Tweed's farmhouse.

"Yes?" the Widow Tweed called, opening the door and looking around. But there was no one to be seen.

Just as she was about to close the door, Big Mama and Dinky flew down and plucked her pink underwear from the clothesline.

"My word!" the Widow Tweed cried. "You come *back* here!"

She ran out of the house after the birds. They dropped her bloomers right near the fence.

As the Widow Tweed picked up her underwear, she was shocked to find a furry little animal huddled in the grass.

"Why, it's a baby fox," she whispered.

She bent down, and the tiny creature uncurled himself and tottered over to her.

Tears came to the Widow Tweed's eyes. "You're such a little toddler," she said, chuckling. "I think I'll call you Tod."

With that, she wrapped him gently in her apron and carried him inside.

Stories About Honesty and Integrity

A Nose for Mischief

from *Pinocchio*

On his way to school one day, the little wooden boy, Pinocchio, met two shady characters who convinced him to join a marionette show. Pinocchio went onstage and thrilled the audience by dancing without strings.

That night, Pinocchio couldn't wait to get home to tell his father, the woodcarver Geppetto, about his performance.

"Home?" said Stromboli the puppeteer, sneering. "Very funny."

He grabbed Pinocchio and tossed him into a birdcage. Then he snapped the padlock shut and left Pinocchio alone in the back of the wagon.

Soon Jiminy Cricket caught up with the wagon and hopped in back. "I should have kept my eye on you," said Jiminy, who had been appointed by the Blue Fairy to be Pinocchio's conscience.

Pinocchio and Jiminy looked out the back of the wagon at the starlit sky. One star blazed and began spinning toward the wagon. The whirling starlight settled in front of Pinocchio's cage, and the Blue Fairy appeared.

"Why, Pinocchio," she said. "Why didn't you go to school?"

"Well, you see," he replied slowly, "I *was* going to school until I met somebody. . . ."

"Met somebody?" said the Blue Fairy.

"Right," continued Pinocchio. "Two big monsters—with big green eyes!"

"Weren't you afraid?" asked the Blue Fairy.

"No, ma'am," said Pinocchio firmly. "But they tied me in a big sack!"

"You don't say . . ." mused the Blue Fairy.

Pinocchio told one lie after another, and each time he lied, his wooden nose grew. It grew and grew, until it poked out of the cage and sprouted leaves. Among the leaves was a bird's nest, with a family of birds!

"Look! My nose!" cried Pinocchio. "What's happening to it?"

"Perhaps you haven't been telling the truth, Pinocchio," said the Blue Fairy. "You see, a lie keeps growing until it's as plain as the nose on your face."

Pinocchio blurted, "I'll never lie again. Honest, I won't!"

"I'll forgive you this once," said the Blue Fairy. "But this is the last time I can help you. Remember, a boy who won't be good might just as well be made of wood."

The Blue Fairy tapped Pinocchio on his nose with her magic wand, then vanished.

Pinocchio's nose returned to normal, and the lock on the cage magically opened. Pinocchio was free to pursue his dream of becoming a real boy. It was a dream that would come true—as long as he remained truthful.

Bianca and Bernard Down Under

from *The Rescuers Down Under*

In the Australian outback, a boy scrambled down the side of a cliff. A poacher, someone who caught and killed wild animals for money, had told him that his friend Marahute, the golden eagle, had been shot. Cody was devastated. He wanted to make sure that the eagle's eggs were safe.

Cody saw the eggs in the nest. "They're still warm!" he said, touching them gently.

As the boy covered the eggs with feathers, a lady mouse appeared at his side. "Cody!" she cried urgently. It was Miss Bianca from the Rescue Aid Society. Along with her partner, Bernard, and a kangaroo mouse named Jake, she wanted to warn Cody that the poacher, McLeach, and his lizard, Joanna, had followed him.

"There's no time to explain," Miss Bianca continued. "You are in grave danger."

Just then Cody saw the golden eagle flying toward the nest. "She's alive!" he cried. "Marahute! It's me!"

Bernard shouted, "McLeach is on the cliff!"

Above them, McLeach sat in his huge poaching machine with his pet lizard, Joanna.

"Marahute!" Cody cried. "Turn back! It's a trap!"

But it was too late. McLeach shot the net over Marahute and captured her. As the bundle swung from the crane, Cody leaped from the ledge and grabbed hold of the net. Jake lassoed Cody's foot and threw the end of the rope to Bernard and Miss Bianca. "Hold tight, you two," Jake cried. "We're going for a ride!"

Miss Bianca caught the rope, but Bernard lost his grip on it. The net swung away from the ledge without him.

McLeach pulled the net up with the crane. Then he dumped Marahute into the cage in the back of the truck, along with Cody, Jake, and Miss Bianca.

As McLeach drove off, Bernard scrambled up the cliff and found a razorback boar to give him a ride. The boar sped off with Bernard on its back, and soon they caught up with McLeach's truck.

At Crocodile Falls, McLeach tied Cody to the end of the crane and dangled him over the rushing water. "You ready, boy?" McLeach cackled. "The crocs love live bait!" McLeach turned a key, and the crane began to lower the rope.

When McLeach wasn't watching, Bernard leaped into the truck and stole the key. The crane immediately stopped. McLeach grabbed his gun and began firing at the rope.

Bernard tossed the keys to Miss Bianca through a hole in the cage. Then he ran full speed toward Joanna and knocked her into McLeach. Both the poacher and the big lizard tumbled into the river. Joanna swam to the opposite bank, while McLeach was swept over the thundering falls.

The rope holding Cody suddenly snapped, and the boy fell into the river. Bernard dived in after him. Then, as Cody was swept over the falls, Marahute swooped down and caught them. On her back rode Jake and Miss Bianca. Thanks to Bernard, the captives had escaped.

The friends soared over the vast Australian outback, free at last.

Small One's Samaritan

from *The Small One: A Good Samaritan*

There was once an old, frail donkey named Small One. He was loved and cared for by a kind man named Joseph, his wife, Mary, and their baby, Jesus.

One day, while looking for a place to rest, he wandered far from the barnyard. Suddenly, he stumbled and fell, rolling down a hill until he came to a stop. His frail body was twisted underneath him and he was cut and bruised. Poor Small One closed his eyes in pain.

At the same time, a boy was walking on the road to Jerusalem. He had been the owner of the old donkey before his father had forced him to sell Small One, since the creature was too weak to do work for them anymore.

When the boy spotted the donkey at the bottom of the hill, he couldn't believe his eyes. "Small One?" he cried. When he came upon the donkey, crumpled and bruised, tears started running down his face. How would he help his old friend?

When the boy saw a man coming down the road and noticed that he was a priest, he felt relief wash over him. He called out, "Holy one! This animal is badly hurt. Can you please help me?"

The priest spoke quickly. "There is nothing you can do for that old, sick donkey. Better to just leave him there." And he hurried off.

The boy could not leave Small One by the side of the road, help-less. Another figure approached. "Please, this animal is badly hurt. Can you help me?"

The man barely glanced their way. He crossed to the other side of the road, as far away as possible, and kept walking.

Then, another figure appeared. This one had a young, strong donkey with him. He stopped by the side of Small One.

"This donkey is badly hurt. Can you help him?" asked the boy again.

The man looked at the boy with kindness in his eyes. "What would

you have me do for this animal?" he asked. "He is very old, and he looks badly injured."

"Do you think you could help me bring Small One to an inn, where he could get better?" the boy asked.

The man replied, "Let us find a way."

Together, the man and the boy fixed up a blanket with some sticks, and gently lifted Small One onto it. In this way, his own strong beast was able to drag the little donkey to an inn.

There, the man helped the boy settle Small One in the stable. Before he left, he gave the boy two silver coins. "Take care of your old friend," he said.

"Wait," said the boy. "Tell me your name! Where are you from?"

"My name does not matter," replied the man. "I am from Samaria."

"Thank you for your kindness," said the boy. "Small One and I will never forget you."

The good Samaritan waved and went on his way.

Ratigan's Revenge

from *The Great Mouse Detective*

During the reign of Queen Mousetoria of England, Basil of Baker Street was trying to find out why the vile and cunning Professor Ratigan had kidnapped a humble toy inventor.

On the day of the Queen's Jubilee, Basil followed Ratigan to Buckingham Palace. He was accompanied by his friend Dr. Dawson, and the inventor's daughter, Olivia. As they entered the throne room, they heard the Queen address her subjects.

"We are here," intoned Her Majesty, "not only to commemorate my sixty years as your queen, but to honor one of truly noble stature. May I present to you Professor Ratigan—my new royal consort!"

As all the mice murmured in shock and dismay, Ratigan stood and read from a scroll. "Thank you, Your Majesty. As your new royal consort, I'm placing a heavy tax on the people who are a burden to society—the ill, the elderly, and little children."

The crowd gasped. Basil knew something was wrong. He searched behind some curtains and found the toy inventer operating a control panel. Ratigan had forced Flaversham to build a robot that looked exactly like the Queen!

Basil grabbed the controls. In the throne room, the robot suddenly pointed at Ratigan. "You low-life scoundrel," the robot said. "You fraud, you impostor, you nincompoop!"

As the crowd hissed, Ratigan grabbed Flaversham's daughter, Olivia. "Stay where you are," he ordered everyone, "or the girl dies!" He carried Olivia outside to a propeller-driven blimp that was waiting for him.

As Ratigan's blimp sailed into the clouds, Basil cried, "Dawson, gather up the helium balloons. Flaversham, fetch me a matchbox." When the materials were gathered, Basil hastily constructed a balloon that could pursue the blimp. Basil, Dawson, and Flaversham leaped into the matchbox, and the balloon soared into the sky.

Soon the balloon caught up with Ratigan's blimp. Basil leaped onto the blimp's rudder. The movement caused Ratigan to lose control of the blimp, and it crashed into the clock tower known as Big Ben.

Basil tumbled into the clockworks. So did Ratigan, still clutching Olivia. Basil chased after Ratigan, then wrested the girl from him.

Basil held Olivia on a narrow ledge and searched the sky for the balloon. "Over here, Dawson!" Basil cried. Dawson manuevered the balloon close to the clock, and Basil quickly handed Olivia to her father.

Just then, Ratigan leaped out and lunged at Basil. He chased Basil through the maze of gears and wheels until he cornered him on the ledge. As Big Ben struck the hour, the bell's powerful vibrations toppled Ratigan and Basil off their feet. They tumbled off the clock tower and disappeared into the clouds.

Suddenly Basil emerged, pedaling the remnants of Ratigan's blimp. Basil was safe. Ratigan was gone. Mr. Flaversham and Olivia were together. And Queen Mousetoria regained the throne, thanks to Basil of Baker Street.

A Fair Fight

from *Peter Pan*

In a pirate ship anchored near the island of Never Land, Captain Hook faced his greatest enemy, Peter Pan. The Captain was furious at Peter for having rescued Wendy, her brothers, and the Lost Boys.

After safely installing the children in the crow's nest, Peter flew down the yardarm.

"Fly! Fly! You coward!" cried Hook.

"Coward?" said Peter. "Me?"

Hook started to climb the rigging. "You wouldn't dare fight old Hook man to man," the Captain taunted. "You'd fly away like a cowardly sparrow."

"Nobody calls me a coward!" Peter replied. "I'll fight you man to man, with one hand tied behind my back!"

Hook joined Peter on the yardarm and locked blades with him. As they stood face-to-face, dagger to sword, Hook said mischievously, "You won't fly?"

Wendy called down from the crow's nest. "Don't do it, Peter! It's a trick."

"I give my word," said Peter.

Hook shouted, "Then let's have at it!"

The duel began. Hook pushed Peter off the yardarm, but Peter grabbed the edge just in time. Peter pulled himself back onto the yardarm, and the fight continued.

As Peter struggled to maintain his balance, Hook knocked the dagger out of Peter's hand. The dagger splashed into the water below. Hook snarled, "Insolent youth—prepare to die!"

"Fly!" Wendy and the boys cried. "Please, Peter, fly!"

"No!" Peter shouted up to them. "I gave my word."

Carefully, Peter felt his way backward along the yardarm. Any second now, he could tumble into the sea or be pierced by the Captain's sword.

As Hook drew back his weapon one last time, Peter looked up and saw a black pirate flag fluttering above the yardarm. Peter jumped up, grabbed the flag, and pulled it down over the Captain's head. While Hook thrashed beneath the banner, Peter seized the captain's sword.

"You're mine, Hook," said Peter triumphantly.

Hook untangled himself from the cloth. He looked down at the sea and saw the crocodile waiting for him. "You wouldn't do old Hook in, now would you, lad?" he said, trembling. "I'll go away forever. I'll do anything you say!"

"All right," Peter said good-humoredly. "Say you're a codfish."

Hook shuddered, horrified.

"Say it!" Peter demanded.

Hook gulped, then said meekly, "I'm a . . . codfish."

"Louder!" Peter demanded.

"I'm a codfish!" Hook screamed. Above him, the boys in the crow's nest began to chant, "Hook is a codfish! Hook is a codfish!"

The Captain was thoroughly humiliated. That blasted Peter Pan had kept his word . . . and beat him!

Mickey's Magical Mix-up

from *The Sorcerer's Apprentice*

Long ago, a powerful sorcerer agreed to take on an apprentice. Day in and day out, the sorcerer busied himself with his spells and incantations while Mickey did all the chores. As Mickey swept the floors, tended the fire, and filled the vat, he dreamed of becoming a sorcerer. He knew he would make a fine magician, if only the sorcerer would stop for a moment and teach him a trick or two. The sorcerer had promised!

Late one night, the sorcerer placed his tall, pointed hat on the table and turned toward the stairs that led to his bedchamber. "When you've filled the vat with water from the fountain, then you, too, may go to bed," said the sorcerer.

"Yes, sir," said Mickey, watching him climb the stairs. Never before had the sorcerer forgotten his enchanted hat!

As soon as he was gone, Mickey ran over to the table and tried on the hat. Instantly Mickey felt that he, too, could make magic. The sorcerer need never find out.

Mickey spied an old straw broom in the corner. Using his new-found powers, he chanted, "*Dooma, dooma, brooma, brooma.*"

The broom sprang to life. Mickey commanded the broom to lift two buckets and follow him to the fountain in the courtyard. The broom filled the buckets with water and marched back to the vat. As soon as the broom finished, Mickey motioned for it to fetch more water.

Quite satisfied, Mickey sat in a comfortable chair and fell asleep. Soon he began to dream. Atop a pinnacle, surrounded by the sea, Mickey raised his arms to command the elements: fire, water, wind, and earth. Shooting stairs whirled around his head. The tides rose higher and higher until they splashed at his feet. He could almost feel the waves tickling his toes. . . .

Mickey awoke abruptly. He was sitting in waist-high water. All along, the broom had continued to fetch the water and fill the vat, and now the room was flooded.

"Stop! Halt!" Mickey cried, but the broom continued. He searched for the sorcerer's book of incantations, but it had disappeared.

In desperation, Mickey grabbed an axe and chopped the broom into pieces. To Mickey's horror, the splinters sprang to life, each holding buckets. Blindly they marched to the fountain and back, filling the vat with water.

The room became a turbulent sea. When the missing book of incantations drifted by, Mickey climbed aboard. Frantically he turned the pages, trying to find a spell that would stop the brooms.

Suddenly the sorcerer threw open the door and murmured the incantation. The waters receded, and Mickey sat, shamefaced, in a puddle. As the sorcerer glared at him, Mickey vowed that he would never make magic again . . . that is, until the sorcerer felt he was ready!

A New Scrooge

from *Mickey's Christmas Carol*

It was Christmas Eve. Bob Cratchit twisted his hands nervously as he faced his employer. Ebenezer Scrooge was never an easy man to deal with.

"A half day off!" shouted Scrooge in disgust. "For Christmas!"

Bob Cratchit looked down. This year seemed worse than ever.

"Go on," Scrooge finally said. "But be here earlier than ever the day after!"

That was how Ebenezer Scrooge treated everyone. He was the richest man in town, but had the coldest heart. Christmas meant nothing to him.

"Bah! Humbug!" Scrooge barked at anyone who wished him a merry Christmas.

That night, Scrooge heard a strange noise. "Who's there?" he called.

Suddenly, the ghost of his old business partner appeared. "It is I, Jacob Marley," the ghost said. "I've come to tell you that tonight you will be visited by three spirits."

Scrooge tried to ignore what the ghost had said. "Humbug!" he said. But as the clock struck midnight, the first spirit appeared.

"I am the ghost of Christmas past," he told Scrooge. Scrooge had no choice but to go with the spirit to see again how he had spent Christmas many years ago. Soon Scrooge saw old friends dancing and singing once more. He even gazed upon the face of Isabel, his old sweetheart.

Scrooge turned away. He knew that he had not been kind to Isabel, or any of the other people the spirit showed him. All he cared about was money.

Before long, another spirit came. "I am the ghost of Christmas present!" the ghost told Scrooge. Once more, Scrooge was carried out of his bed and into the snowy streets of London. He looked into the window of the tiny, poor home of Bob Cratchit.

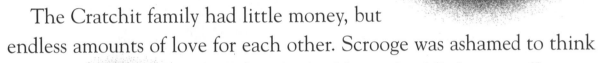

The Cratchit family had little money, but endless amounts of love for each other. Scrooge was ashamed to think of how he had begrudged Bob time off to spend with his young son, Tiny Tim.

There was little time to think of that, though, for suddenly the final spirit appeared. "I suppose you are the ghost of Christmas yet to come," Scrooge said. In a puff of wind, he found himself in a lonely graveyard.

"Spirit, why do you bring me here?" Scrooge asked in a frightened voice. Then he saw a lonely tombstone before him—IT WAS HIS OWN!

Scrooge shouted, "I will change! I will be a better duck! I will keep Christmas in my heart all year long!" Then he realized he was awake and safe in his own bed. "It's Christmas!" he cried, jumping out of bed. He knew what he had to do. He ran over to Bob Cratchit's house.

"Merry Christmas!" Scrooge shouted as he pounded on the door. He had brought a huge bag of toys for the children.

"God bless us, every one," Tiny Tim said. And Scrooge couldn't have agreed more.

Mirror, Mirror on the Wall

from *Snow White and the Seven Dwarfs*

 nce upon a time, a very beautiful but cruel queen owned a magic mirror. Every time she looked into it, she asked the same thing:

> *"Magic mirror on the wall,*
> *Who is the fairest one of all?"*

The mirror always answered that she was the fairest in the land, until one day it replied:

> *"Famed is thy beauty, Majesty. But hold—a lovely maid I see!*
> *Alas she is more fair than thee!"*

The vain queen knew at once that the mirror spoke of the Princess Snow White. The Queen vowed that the Princess must die.

Using her evil magic, the Queen transformed herself into an ugly old beggar woman. In her disguise, she went out to the forest where Snow White lived in hiding. Hanging on her arm was a basket of poisoned apples.

Snow White was not alone in the forest. She lived in the cottage of the seven dwarfs—Doc, Happy, Sleepy, Sneezy, Bashful, Grumpy, and Dopey. They loved her gentle goodness and vowed to protect her from the wicked queen. Each day, before they left to work in the diamond mine, they warned Snow White to be careful.

Snow White knew that the Queen wanted to harm her, but she had no idea that the beggar woman who came to the cottage was her enemy! She kindly invited her inside.

"Hello, dearie," croaked the old woman. "Would you like to try one of my delicious apples?"

The forest birds and animals tried to warn Snow White, but it was too late. She took a bite of an apple and fell down in a deep sleep.

"Now *I* am the fairest in the land!" shrieked the hag.

The animals raced through the woods to the diamond mine. The dwarfs hurried back to their cottage and chased the wicked queen up a mountain. Suddenly, a bolt of lightning struck the rock where the Queen stood, and she fell from the cliff, never to be seen again.

The dwarfs promised that they would never again leave Snow White's side. They stood guard beside her throughout the year, night and day, until one day, a young prince rode up.

The Prince recognized Snow White as the young woman he had once loved. Gently, he leaned over and kissed her. Snow White's eyes opened. The spell was broken at last!

And they all lived happily ever after.

Hook Hatches a Plan

from *Peter Pan*

Tinker Bell was a jealous little pixie. Her friend Peter Pan was spending all his time with his new friend, Wendy, and Tinker Bell was afraid he didn't care for her anymore. Every time she tried to make that awful Wendy-girl go away, Peter foiled Tink's plan and rescued her.

If only that Wendy would just go away! Tinker Bell thought angrily.

At that moment, Captain Hook was trying to think of a way to be rid of Peter Pan forever. "If I only knew where his secret hideout was," he said. He decided to bring Tinker Bell to his ship and trick her into telling him.

"I will make Wendy go away forever," Captain Hook promised Tinker Bell. "But you must show me where Peter Pan lives so I can find her."

Tinker Bell happily showed Captain Hook Hangman's Tree on a map. With a delighted laugh, the evil pirate grabbed Tinker Bell and threw her into a lantern. Tinker Bell realized that she had been fooled, and now Peter was in danger!

"I won't lay a hook on Pan," Captain Hook promised. "This little present will do the job for me." Captain Hook sent a box to Peter Pan, and hidden inside was a bomb about to explode!

Tinker Bell knew she had to rescue Peter Pan. She pushed with all her might against the side of the lantern until it tipped over. Tinker Bell slipped out and flew as fast as she could to Hangman's Tree.

"Hi, Tink!" Peter called. "I was just about to open this present!"

Tinker Bell zoomed down, grabbed the box from Peter's hands, and whisked it away. Within seconds, the bomb exploded. Rocks and trees flew all about as the island shook from the blast.

"Good-bye, Peter Pan," Captain Hook said as he watched the explosion from his ship.

But Tinker Bell had saved Peter Pan. Just as the present exploded, she had pushed him to safety.

"Tink?" Peter Pan called. Under a big pile of rocks, a faint light glowed. "Tink, are you all right? You have to be all right! What would I do without you?" Peter Pan began to toss the rocks aside to rescue his dear friend.

Suddenly, Tinker Bell knew she had no reason to be jealous of Wendy. Peter Pan cared about her, after all. Knowing this, she began to feel better. Together the friends went off to foil Captain Hook's wicked plans once more.

The Queen's Quick Temper

from *Alice in Wonderland*

Alice was quite lost. She had followed the White Rabbit down his rabbit hole, and from there on she had no idea where she was. No matter which way she went, the most unusual things happened to her. But she kept wandering through the woods until she heard some voices singing.

Perhaps they'll be able to tell me how to get home, Alice thought as she hurried into a formal garden.

Three gardeners were busy dabbing all the white roses on a tree with red paint. It was an odd thing for them to do, but Alice had seen many odd things on her journey.

"Why are you painting the roses red?" she asked them.

The three gardeners explained that they had planted white roses by mistake. The Queen wanted only red ones, and her temper was fierce. They were certain that she would chop off their heads if she found out.

"It's a wicked temper she has," they whispered fearfully to Alice.

"Oh, dear!" Alice cried. "Let me help you!"

Alice climbed a ladder and began to paint the white roses red, too. Suddenly a trumpet blasted. The Queen was coming!

Alice and the gardeners bowed down before the Queen. They trembled in fright as she approached. Just as they had feared, the Queen noticed the red paint at once!

"Who's been painting my roses red?" she roared. "The ace? The deuce? Off with their heads! Off with their heads!"

Everyone ducked as the Queen ranted and raged. Her face grew red and her loud voice echoed across the garden. Alice was terrified. She had never seen anyone with such a bad temper!

Just then the King, a meek little man, begged the Queen to let Alice and the gardeners have a trial. To everyone's surprise, the Queen agreed.

Alice watched in shock as the mischievous Cheshire Cat appeared. He winked at Alice. "Let's get her really mad, shall we?" he said with a grin.

"Oh, no!" Alice cried. The queen's rage was even worse than she had imagined. Soon the Queen was shouting for everyone's head to be chopped off. It seemed there was no pleasing her that day.

Alice put her apron over her head to hide from the Queen's anger. In her pocket was a piece of the magic mushroom that had made her grow taller. Quickly she took a bite.

To the shock of everyone in the court, Alice grew and grew, right before their eyes.

"All people a mile high must leave!" shouted the Queen.

And so Alice left, running as fast as she could from the upside-down world of Wonderland and the Queen's quick temper!

The Small One

from *The Small One*

Long ago, there was a boy who lived near the town of Nazareth. His father owned four donkeys to help with the chores. Three of the beasts were young and strong, but the fourth, who was smaller than the others, was old and weak. The boy took care of all the donkeys, but he loved Small One best of all. Small One was his friend.

One day, the boy and his father were gathering firewood. They loaded the heavy logs on the donkeys' backs. The boy tried to find the lightest pieces of wood for Small One to carry, for he knew that the donkey was too weak to carry a heavy burden.

"Don't you have enough work to do without doing Small One's, too?" his father asked.

"Oh, Father. He is no trouble at all. I don't mind," the boy said.

"Son," his father said. "Small One is old. His strength is gone. We cannot afford to keep him any longer."

The boy grabbed his father's arm. "No!" he pleaded. "You can't mean it!"

"Please, son," his father said, "try to understand. Small One is old. He should not have to work so hard. In town he will have an easier life. You must be strong."

"Yes, Father," the boy replied, but he felt as if his heart would break.

The little donkey, too, was very sad. But the boy tried to cheer him up.

"Don't worry, Small One," he said. "I won't sell you to just anyone. He will be someone special, someone who will love you as I do."

The next morning, the boy and Small One walked over the hills to Nazareth.

At the town gates they were stopped by a guard who demanded to know their business. "I have come to sell my donkey, sir," the boy explained.

The guard looked at Small One and laughed. "I know a man who is in need of such an animal," he said. "Go to the third shop inside these gates."

The boy thanked the guard profusely, but when they reached the shop, his heart grew cold. Inside, a man was sharpening a knife. Several animals were tied up, and they looked frightened.

The man offered the boy a piece of silver—for Small One's hide!

The boy and Small One ran away as fast as they could. "I'm sorry, Small One," the boy said when they were a safe distance from the tanner's shop.

From place to place they roamed, but no one wanted to buy Small One. Night was coming.

The tired donkey knew that only one man would buy him. He led the boy back to the tanner's shop, ready to give up his life to help his friend.

The boy sat down beside Small One and began to cry.

Suddenly, the boy felt a hand on his shoulder. He looked up into the eyes of a man.

"Tell me, son," the man said. "Is your donkey for sale? I need a gentle beast to carry my wife, Mary, to Bethlehem."

"Yes, sir," he said.

"What do you call him?" the man asked.

"Small One," replied the boy.

"Well, he looks strong enough," said the man.

"And kind," said the boy.

The man smiled. "I can offer you only one piece of silver," he said. "I know it is very little."

"Oh, that's fine!" the boy cried. "I just want Small One to have a good home."

"He will," said the man. "I'll take good care of him."

As the man, his wife, and Small One disappeared down the road toward Bethlehem, the boy watched from a hilltop and waved good-bye.

The boy was sad, but also happy. For he knew that Small One had found a good home at last.

Marley's Mistakes

from Mickey's Christmas Carol

ate one Christmas Eve, Scrooge made his way home. The wind moaned down the deserted streets and the snow swirled around him.

Scrooge reached his dark house and gazed up at the door. The knocker was carved in the likeness of a lion's head. But tonight, it began to change shape right before his eyes. It looked exactly like his

dead business partner, Jacob Marley! Scrooge couldn't believe his eyes. Suddenly an unearthly voice broke the silence. *"Ehhhbeneezer Scroooge!"*

Scrooge looked around frantically. But the voice was coming from the knocker—from Marley's head!

"Jacob Marley?" Scrooge whispered. "No! It can't be!"

Scrooge yanked open the door and dashed inside. He ran up the stairs and into his bedroom. He slammed the door behind him and bolted all the locks. He heaved a sigh of relief. But a moment later, there was a loud knock on the door.

"Ehhhbeneezer Scroooge!" the voice moaned again.

There was nowhere to hide. Scrooge pulled his hat down over his frightened eyes.

"Go away!" he cried.

But Scrooge could hear the sound of chains being dragged across the floor. He turned around and shivered to the bone. "Jacob Marley! It *is* you!"

"*Ebenezer,*" the ghost moaned. "Remember when I robbed the widows and swindled the poor?"

For a moment, Scrooge forgot his fright. "Yes!" he cried. "You were brilliant!"

"No," said the ghost, "I was wrong. And so, as punishment, I'm forced to carry these heavy chains throughout eternity. I'm doomed!" The ghost waved its arms around in despair. "And the same thing will happen to you, Ebenezer Scrooge!"

"No!" Scrooge cried. "It can't! It mustn't! Help me, Jacob!"

But the ghost was deaf to Scrooge's pleas. "Tonight," it declared, "you will be visited by three spirits. Listen to them. Do what they say, or your chains will be even heavier than mine!"

And with that the ghost disappeared, leaving the miserable Scrooge shaking in his chair.

Poor, Unfortunate Souls

from *The Little Mermaid*

rsula was a sea witch who lived in the darkest corner of the sea, and she was as ugly as she was evil. For many years she had dwelt below the waves, tricking merpeople into giving up their souls.

Triton, king of the merpeople, had banished Ursula from his kingdom years ago, and she was bent on revenge.

One day, the demon gazed into her crystal ball, and she saw Ariel. Ursula sneered at the lovesick look on the girl's face. She now knew

the key to Ariel's heart. More than anything, Ariel wanted to be with Eric, a human.

"Oh, it's too easy!" Ursula sniggered. "The child is in love with a human. And not just any human—a prince! Her daddy will *love* that!"

Ursula threw back her head and cackled with glee. She danced around her collection of shivering, sad-eyed souls—all trapped in her garden of evil.

Each tiny, distorted body had once been a merperson—a merperson so fraught with desire that he or she had been willing to strike a deal with the evil Ursula. But the deals always ended in misery and unfulfilled dreams. Ursula saw to that, for she was anything but fair.

And Ursula vowed to add Ariel to her collection.

But Eric's love for Ariel was stronger than his fear of death. He attacked the powerful Ursula armed only with a harpoon. And though the Sea Witch let all her vast evil swell her to the size of a living mountain, Eric steered his battered ship straight at her, and its broken mast pierced her belly.

Ursula's cry of pain blotted out the sound of thunder. She sank like an island, disappearing forever. Ariel was free, and so were all the poor, unfortunate souls.

Dodger Sneaks a Snack

from *Oliver & Company*

R ita, a leggy hound with long, silky ears, gazed sadly out the window. Suddenly she brightened. "Here comes Dodger!" she cried. "Maybe he's had some luck."

A friendly mutt with a lopsided grin strutted into the shabby room. He was wearing a string of hot dogs around his neck. "Cool it, Dodger fans," he announced. "I'd like to introduce you to . . . dinner! Hot dogs à la Dodger!"

Francis the bulldog was so happy to see food that he could barely maintain his composure. "Thank you, Dodger," he said. "You remain our preeminent benefactor."

"Yeah, and you're okay, too," added Einstein, the gangly old Great Dane. "How did you do it?"

"Well," bragged Dodger, "let me tell you. It was tough! Only *I* could've done it. Picture the city—Eighth and Broadway. Crowds are hustling. Hot dogs are sizzling. Enter Dodger, one bad puppy. Then along comes a greedy, ugly psychotic monster with razor-sharp claws, dripping fangs and—"

Dodger's story was interrupted. An orange kitten fell through the rotting roof and landed in the midst of the dogs. The kitten was terrified.

"I—I followed a dog here," he stammered. "I . . . I just wanted some of the hot dogs I helped him get."

"Hey, kitty," Dodger said. "What took you so long?"

Francis sized up the kitten. "I assume this is the psychotic monster you were talking about."

"Come on, Dodger," jeered Tito the chihuahua. "Let's see this big, bad kitty in action."

Rita nuzzled the shivering kitten. "Enough kidding around, guys. He's so little. I wonder where his mother is."

"You got a name, cat?" Tito asked.

The kitten shook his head. "I was left for adoption in a box. My brothers were all taken yesterday. Then Dodger came along. He said we'd be pals."

"We will be, kid," Dodger reassured him. "Now, dig in!"

Stories About Love and Friendship

The Trouble with Tiggers

from *Winnie the Pooh and Tigger Too*

Rabbit was tired of being bounced by Tigger—bounced and trounced and knocked down by Tigger. So he was quite happy when he and his friends found Tigger and Roo stuck up in a tree.

"Tigger can't bounce anybody as long as he's stuck up in that tree," Rabbit said cheerfully.

"We can't just leave them up there," said Christopher Robin. "We have to get them both down. Now, everyone take hold of my coat. Ready? Okay, you're first, Roo. Jump!"

"Here I come!" Roo cried, letting go of the branch. "Whee!"

Roo landed safely in the middle of Christopher Robin's coat. "That was fun!" cried Roo. "Come on, Tigger. Jump!"

Tigger frowned and clung tighter to his branch. "Jump? Tiggers don't jump. They bounce."

"Then why don't you bounce down?" said Pooh.

"Tiggers only bounce *up*," replied Tigger.

Christopher Robin sighed. "Then you'll have to *climb* down."

"Tiggers can't climb down because . . . because their tails get in the way." Tigger wrapped his tail around the tree trunk to prove his point.

Suddenly Rabbit came up with a solution. "If Tigger won't jump down or climb down," Rabbit proclaimed, "we'll just have to leave him up there forever!"

Tigger didn't like the sound of *forever*, but he said, rather sadly, "If I ever get down from this tree, I promise never to bounce again."

Rabbit did a little jig in the snow. "Did you all hear that?" he said gleefully. "Tigger promised never to bounce again!"

Tigger slowly unwound his tail from the tree trunk and looked down. With a bit of coaxing from his friends below, Tigger ever so carefully climbed down from the tree.

As Tigger stood in the snow, Rabbit reminded him, "You promised!"

"Not even one teensy-weensy bounce?" Tigger asked.

"Not even a *smidgen* of a bounce," replied Rabbit.

Tigger hung his head and trudged off into the woods, his tail dragging behind him.

Roo said to Christopher Robin, "I like the old bouncy Tigger best."

Christopher Robin agreed, as did Pooh and Piglet and Kanga. They all looked at Rabbit.

"Well, I . . ." Rabbit fumbled. Didn't his friends remember how annoying it was to be bounced by Tigger? He guessed not, because they all looked as droopy as Tigger.

"Oh, all right," said Rabbit. "I guess I like the old Tigger better, too."

Tigger had been listening nearby. He bounced up to Rabbit and knocked him into the snow. "Come on, Rabbit," Tigger cried. "Let's bounce together!"

A Different Kind of Friendship

from *The Fox and the Hound*

ne day, a young fox and a young hound met in the woods. Neither knew that foxes and hounds were not supposed to get along.

"I'm a fox," said one. "My name's Tod. What's your name?"

"Mine's Copper. I'm a hound dog!"

"Gee," said Tod. "I bet you'd be good at playing hide-and-seek. Want to try it, Copper?"

All afternoon the fox and hound played together. Before they headed home, Tod said, "You're my best friend, Copper."

"And you're mine, too, Tod."

Copper grinned. "And we'll always be friends, forever. Won't we?"

"Yeah, forever!" replied Tod.

Copper lived with an old dog called Chief and a hunter named Amos Slade. Tod lived with Widow Tweed, a kindhearted woman who took him in after he had lost his mother.

As the months passed, Amos took Copper into the woods and taught him how to hunt. Widow Tweed kept Tod at home, where he would be safe from Amos and other hunters.

One night, Tod sneaked out to visit Copper.

"You have to go, Tod!" said Copper. "'I'm a hunting dog now. And you'd better get out of here before Chief wakes up."

Chief heard them. He chased Tod onto a railroad trestle. A train sped toward them, and Tod flattened himself between the rails. Chief was knocked off the trestle into a ravine below. He survived, but was injured.

Tod crept home to Widow Tweed's.

Widow Tweed learned about the accident from Amos. The very next day, Widow Tweed took Tod to a wildlife refuge.

Amos was still angry at Tod for having caused Chief's injuries. With Copper beside him, Amos went to the wildlife refuge to catch the young fox.

When Amos and Copper saw Tod, they pursued him through the woods. Tod could not believe that his friend Copper was chasing him.

As Tod dashed through the undergrowth, a huge bear lumbered out of the woods and swiped at Amos and Copper.

Tod turned and saw the bear towering over his old friend. He leaped on the bear's back and bit him, then lured the bear to the river and onto a fallen log. The log snapped, and both animals tumbled into the water. While the bear lay unconscious, Tod swam to the riverbank.

Amos stood on the bank with a gun. As the hunter took aim, Copper jumped in front of Tod. The fox had just saved their lives!

Amos thought a moment, then lowered the gun.

Soon after, Copper and Tod said good-bye to each other. They were adults now, and their lives had changed. Yet in their hearts they would remain friends forever.

3-2-1 Blastoff!

from *Toy Story*

Buzz and Woody, two of Andy's toys, had been captured by his cruel neighbor, Sid. They were abandoned in Sid's room filled with mutant toys—scary-looking creatures made from different toy parts.

Luckily, Sid had left his bedroom door open.

"We're free!" Woody cried.

Woody and Buzz hurried out the door. In another room, Buzz saw a TV ad for Buzz Lightyear toys. Shocked, he tried to fly, but crashed at the bottom of the stairs, and one of his arms snapped off.

Woody picked up Buzz's arm and dragged Buzz back to Sid's room. Suddenly the mutant toys grabbed Buzz's arm and surrounded him. Then they backed away.

"Hey, Buzz!" cried Woody.

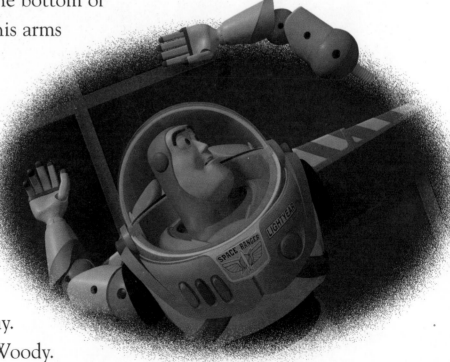

"They fixed your arm! Well, what do you know—these guys are on our side."

Just then Sid ran into the room. The boy dropped his toolbox on a crate, trapping Woody underneath.

"Now," Sid said, "what'll I blow up?" He spied Buzz and cried, "To infinity and beyond!" Quickly he strapped a rocket to the toy's back. Then it began to rain, and Sid had to wait another day.

That night, after Sid had fallen asleep, Woody whispered to Buzz, "Hey! See if you can get this toolbox off the crate, will ya? Then I'll get that rocket thing off you."

"Who cares if I get blown up?" Buzz replied sadly. "I'm just a toy."

"Whoa, hey!" said Woody. "There's a kid next door who thinks you're the greatest. And it's not because you're a space ranger, it's because you're a toy. *His* toy."

Buzz stood up and pushed the toolbox off the crate. Woody wriggled free. Then they had a new problem. The sun was rising.

Sid woke up, grabbed Buzz, and headed downstairs. Woody begged the mutant toys for help. "Please," said Woody. "He's my friend."

Woody and the mutant toys hurried outside. As Sid was about to light the rocket, the mutant toys marched toward the boy. "We don't like being blown up or smashed or ripped to shreds," Woody shouted. "So, from now on—play nice!"

Sid had never heard his toys talk. He screamed and tore off for the house.

By working together, the toys had escaped!

Oliver on His Own

from *Oliver & Company*

One day a copper-colored kitten was left on a street corner, hungry and alone. He tried to sneak sausages from a vendor with the help of a stray dog named Dodger, but Dodger snatched the sausages and ran away.

The kitten followed Dodger to an abandoned barge. There he met some other dogs and their master, a good-hearted thief named Fagin.

He seemed happy to see the kitten. He scratched him under his chin and said, "We've never had a kitten in our gang before. We need all the help we can get!"

The kitten wondered if he had finally found a home, but he wasn't quite sure what kind of life he would have with Fagin and the gang. Fagin owed a great deal of money to Sykes, a vicious man with two Doberman pinschers.

The next day, Fagin sent the gang out to find some loot. As the kitten and Tito, a fast-talking Chihuahua, tried to take a stereo from a limousine, the kitten got trapped in the car with a little girl, Jenny. She seemed as lonely as the kitten. Her parents were away on a trip, and she had just learned that they wouldn't be home in time for her birthday.

Jenny hugged the kitten and said, "Poor little kitty. I'm going to take you home."

Jenny fed the kitten and gave him a warm bed to sleep in. She also gave him a name: Oliver. Jenny took Oliver to a jewelry shop and had a gold tag engraved with his name and address on it.

Just as Oliver was getting used to his new life, Fagin's gang grabbed him and took him back to the barge.

"I was happy there," Oliver moaned. "Why did you guys take me?"

"What do you mean, kid?" asked Dodger. "You're part of our gang. Hey, this place not good enough for you anymore?" he said, sounding hurt.

Oliver struggled to explain. "No, I like everyone in the gang. But there was a little girl, and . . . Dodger, I just want to go back!"

Just then Fagin saw the gold tag around Oliver's neck. He assumed that Oliver's owner was terribly rich, so he wrote a ransom note. But when Jenny appeared with her piggy bank, Fagin didn't have the heart to take it from her.

As Fagin was handing Oliver over to Jenny, Sykes pulled up in his big car and grabbed the little girl. He would demand a ransom from her parents!

After a wild chase, Fagin and the gang rescued Jenny. The little girl was so grateful that she invited the whole gang over to her house to celebrate her birthday. Afterward, Oliver followed Dodger outside.

"Thanks for everything, Dodger."

Dodger replied, "Take care of yourself, kid. And if you ever need anything, you'll know where to find me."

elle was locked away in the Beast's castle, lonely and frightened. She had agreed to stay at the castle so that her father could be free. Now she was alone and feeling very sad.

Quietly she peeked out her door. The Beast was nowhere in sight. Holding her breath, Belle tiptoed along the long hallway and down the curved staircase. A light shone from the kitchen.

Belle decided things couldn't get much worse, so she bravely pushed the door of the kitchen open.

"Good evening, mademoiselle!" cried Lumiere, the candlestick. He rushed forward to take Belle's hand. Then he bowed deeply and kissed it.

"Well, look who's here!" declared Mrs. Potts cheerfully. "What can we get for you, love?"

Belle began to feel a little better. They might be household objects, but their smiles were bright and they seemed anxious to make her feel at home.

"Well, I am a little hungry," Belle admitted.

That was all they needed to hear. Suddenly the room was alive with activity as forks and spoons leaped from the drawers, and dishes and glasses rolled from the cabinets. Belle found herself being led into the dining room as tantalizing dishes danced past her: breads, stews, vegetables, meats. And the desserts—pies and cakes and puddings and pastries! Fruits and drinks of every kind presented themselves. Belle began to clap in the excitement of it all.

Mrs. Potts bustled about, happy to show off her skills. Cogsworth felt very important directing all the dishes and foods in Belle's direction. And charming Lumiere made sure Belle's every wish was granted.

The grand show went on and on. Everyone wanted to do something to welcome their guest. Belle was dazzled by all the trouble

everyone went to to make sure she was happy. The room rocked with the singing and dancing of every pot, pan, and plate in the castle. Even the napkins swirled like ballerinas.

At last Belle's meal was finished. "Bravo!" she exclaimed, jumping from her seat to applaud.

Lumiere, Cogsworth, and Mrs. Potts smiled modestly. "Oh, it was nothing," they said.

But it was something very special indeed. Belle knew that her new friends had risked the Beast's anger just to make her feel welcome. For the first time, Belle began to have hope that maybe things would work out all right, after all!

The Greatest Sacrifice

from *Hercules*

uring his stay in Thebes, Hercules had fallen in love with a young woman named Megara. He had trusted her completely, until he found out that Meg was in league with Hades, the ruler of the Underworld.

"It's not like you think!" Meg pleaded with Hercules. "I mean, I couldn't . . ." She stifled a sob. "I . . . I'm so sorry."

Hercules did not want to listen. He was so heartbroken he could hardly move. And to think, he had traded his incredible godlike strength to save Meg from Hades!

Taking advantage of Hercules' weakness, Hades set Thebes on fire and sent a one-eyed monster to destroy the hero. But Hercules didn't even bother to fight back. He let the city burn and allowed the Cyclops to pummel him.

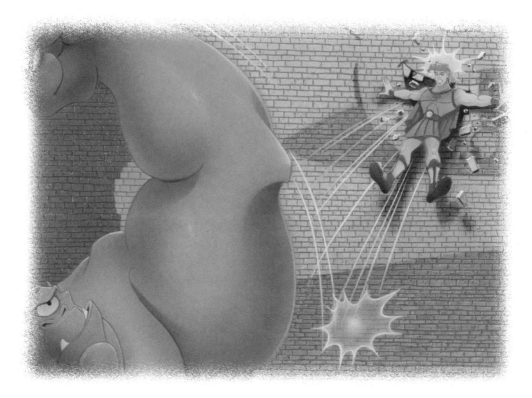

Meg hurried up to him. "Without your strength," she cried, "you'll be killed!"

"There are worse things," replied Hercules in a flat, resigned voice.

Meg could not stand by and watch Hercules be killed. She leaped on the back of Hercules' flying horse, Pegasus, and told him to find Philoctetes, Hercules' former trainer.

They found Phil at the docks. "Herc needs your help!" Meg cried.

Phil wouldn't even look at her. "Why does he need me when he has friends like *you*?" he spat.

"He won't listen to me!" Meg replied.

"Good! He's finally learned something."

Meg wailed, "If you don't help him, Phil, he'll die!"

Phil agreed to help. With Meg, he arrived just in time to see the Cyclops dash Hercules against a pillar. "Come on, kid, fight back!" Phil cried.

Herc glanced at Meg, then focused a swollen eye on the trainer. "You were right all along, Phil. Dreams are for rookies."

"No, kid. Giving up is for rookies. I'm not quittin'. How about you?"

Hercules considered Phil's words. Then he jumped up, grabbed a burning stick, and thrust it at the monster's eye. As the Cyclops

thrashed about, howling, Hercules hastily tied a rope around the giant's ankles. The Cyclops tripped on the rope and knocked against two marble columns. As the columns wobbled, the monster plunged into the sea.

One of the pillars fell toward Hercules. "Look out!" Meg cried. She ran to Hercules and pushed him out of the way, only to have the column crash down on her.

"Meg!" Hercules pushed against the column, sweating and straining. Suddenly his godlike strength returned, and Hercules lifted up the column without any effort.

He bent down and cradled Meg in his strong arms.

"You . . . ," he said, catching his breath. "You saved me. But why?"

"I guess people do crazy things when they're in love."

"Love? Oh, Meg . . . Meg . . . I, I . . ."

"Are you always this articulate?" Meg grinned weakly at him. "You can still stop Hades, but there isn't much time."

Baloo Lends a Paw

from *The Jungle Book*

Baloo the bear loved Mowgli more than any other animal in the jungle. He taught Mowgli all about the bare necessities of life. Sometimes he even forgot that Mowgli was really a mancub, and not a bear at all. So when Bagheera, the panther, reminded Baloo that Mowgli's place was in the village with the other men, Baloo felt very sad.

But Baloo knew that Bagheera was right. The cunning tiger, Shere Khan, was just waiting for his chance to pounce on the boy. The

sooner Mowgli was safely among his own kind, the better. But when Baloo tried to explain this to Mowgli, the boy got very angry.

"I'm not a man, I'm a bear, like you," he told Baloo.

Baloo scratched his head. He just wasn't very good at explaining things. "Now look, Mowgli. You've got to go back and that's all there is to it."

Mowgli stamped his foot. "I'm not going!" he shouted, and he dashed into the jungle.

Baloo ran after him, but the heavy bear was far too slow to catch up to the little boy. Mowgli was gone.

Mowgli roamed the jungle on his own. He didn't care what anyone said. The mancub was sure he could take care of himself just fine.

Suddenly a pair of hypnotic eyes entranced him. Kaa, the snake, had caught Mowgli in his coils! He was all set to make a meal out of the boy when a cold voice interrupted him.

"Give the mancub to me, Kaa!" snarled Shere Khan. "Not so fast, Shere Khan!" shouted a familiar voice. It was Baloo!

"Get this kid out of here," Baloo ordered. A group of vultures swooped down and carried Mowgli to safety.

Mowgli watched as Baloo fought with Shere Khan. Even the vultures were hoping Baloo would win. Baloo fought bravely for his little friend, but the tiger seemed to be winning.

A bolt of lightning struck a nearby tree. "Fire!" shouted the vultures. "Shere Khan is afraid of it!"

Mowgli quickly grabbed a burning branch and tied it the the tiger's tail. Shere Khan howled as the flames burned his fur, and raced away, never to be seen again.

Mowgli sighed in relief. He was safe, thanks to the vultures and his loyal friend, Baloo the bear.

Christmas in the Castle

from *Beauty and the Beast: The Enchanted Christmas*

It was Christmas Eve. Belle looked outside at the falling snow. She was a prisoner in the Beast's castle, but lately she had been happier about living there. The Beast seemed kinder, and she had begun to feel fond of him.

"Let's surprise the Beast!" she said to Lumiere, the candlestick. "We'll decorate the castle for Christmas!"

"No, no, no!" declared Cogsworth, the clock. "The master has forbidden Christmas."

Lumiere frowned at the stuffy clock and then smiled at Belle. "What a wonderful idea, mademoiselle!"

As Belle and her new friends bustled about the castle decorating, Belle had another idea. "I will give the Beast a Christmas present," she told Cogsworth and Lumiere.

"Oh, no!" cried Cogsworth. "That would be a dreadful mistake!" He remembered that the Beast hated Christmas gifts. He had been turned into a Beast by an enchantress after sneering at her gift the year before.

But Belle's mind was made up. Christmas wouldn't be Christmas without presents, and she was sure the Beast would be happy to receive one.

"WHAT?!!!" thundered the Beast when he heard about the Christmas preparations. "HOW DARE SHE?!!!" He stormed through the west wing of the castle, stomping his feet in rage. He HATED Christmas!

Lumiere watched the Beast throw a temper tantrum. Then he called out, "Sir, there's a present here. It's for you."

The Beast stopped in his tracks. "A present?"

Lumiere grinned. "It's from a *girl!*" he said.

The Beast wrinkled his brow. "Mrs. Potts?" he asked.

Lumiere clucked. "No, no, no! It's from Belle!"

The Beast approached the present curiously, all his anger gone. Imagine, Belle had given him a Christmas present! He began to tear it open.

"Ah, ah, ah, Monsieur," Lumiere said. " You can't open it now. You have to wait until Christmas."

The Beast grumbled. "But I don't have anything for her," he realized.

Lumiere put an arm around his master. "You still have time to get her something," he told him. "Something romantic! Something to impress her!" Lumiere wanted more than anything for the Beast and Belle to fall in love so that the spell over the castle would be broken.

The Beast listened to his old friend. He liked Belle, and wanted desperately to please her. At last he had an idea.

"I'll ask Forte to compose a song for her. A pretty, happy song," he decided. He was glad to have come up with such a perfect solution. For the first time, the Beast was beginning to feel the spirit of Christmas in his heart.

Stick Together

from *Toy Story*

oody the cowboy stood up tall in his cowboy boots, waving his arms to make the other toys notice him.

"Attention! Attention everyone!" he shouted. The noisy toys lined up in front of him. They were all very nervous and excited. Today was moving day!

"All right, now that everyone is here, let's get started," Woody said. "We have to stick together to make sure no one gets left behind in the move. So we each have to pick a moving partner."

"Howdy, pardner," joked a rubber chicken.

"It's not funny," said Woody. "Now, I'll pick . . . Bo Peep."

Nobody was surprised. Woody and Bo were sweethearts.

The rest of the toys had a harder time choosing partners. Rex the dinosaur was so worried about being left behind, he chose one hundred moving buddies! All of them were little green soldiers. Rex felt safer with them.

All the toys started arguing about who would be pairing up.

"Everybody calm down," Woody shouted over the din. But just then, Andy burst through the door. All the toys froze where they were.

Andy began tossing toys into a box. Downstairs, his mother called for him to hurry up.

Woody glanced under the bed. A teddy bear waved back. As soon as Andy's back was turned, Woody pushed the bear into the light.

"Mom, I found Molly's bear!" Andy yelled, tossing it into the box. He was searching through the toys. "Hey, Mom! I can't find Buzz!" Andy shouted.

The toys looked at one another. Buzz Lightyear, the spaceman, was one of Andy's favorite toys. They all thought he had been packed already!

Woody was beginning to panic. He couldn't just leave his friend behind! Suddenly, the answer came to him. Andy always took a toy with him when he delivered newspapers on his bicycle. Buzz must be in the bike basket!

Soon all the toys were packed and loaded into the car. Woody peeked out of the box. Andy's bike was strapped to the back of the car, but there was no sign of Buzz. Woody told Bo he had to switch partners. Carefully, he climbed out of the car and slid into the bike basket.

"Howdy, moving partner!" he told a surprised Buzz Lightyear. "Permission to come aboard?"

Together, the friends rode to their new home.

A Lovely Bella Notte

from *Lady and the Tramp*

ady, a pretty cocker spaniel from the nice side of town, was a bit nervous. She was not at all sure if she should trust Tramp. But the stray had saved her life.

"Hey!" Tramp cried, struck by a great idea. "Let's go to Tony's! The perfect place for a special occasion. Come on."

Lady followed Tramp to a restaurant that glowed with candlelight. Delicious smells wafted out, and Lady could hear someone singing. Entranced, she started toward the front door.

"No!" Tramp whispered. "This way. I have my own private entrance."

He turned down a dark alley.

Lady hesitated. The alley looked scary. But she couldn't back out now.

"Wait here," Tramp instructed.

Lady hid behind a garbage can and watched Tramp scratch on the restaurant's backdoor.

A moment later, a big, friendly-looking man wearing an apron opened the door.

"Hello, Butch!" he said. "Where you been, huh?"

The man seemed very happy to see him. Tramp licked his face.

"Hey, Joe," the man yelled into the restaurant. "Bring some bones for Butch before he eats me up."

"Okay, Tony," Joe called. "Some bones coming right up."

Tramp seemed a little disappointed. Truth was, he was hoping for more elegant fare.

He ran over to Lady and barked loudly.

"What's this?" Tony asked. Then he saw Lady and smiled.

"Hey, Joe," Tony shouted. "Butch has a new girlfriend."

Tony scratched Lady under the jaw and all her nervousness disappeared.

He went back into the restaurant, and in a moment returned with a small table covered with a red-and-white checkered tablecloth. He put down breadsticks and a candle.

For us? Lady marveled. She had never been allowed to dine at the table before.

The couple sat down. Tramp studied the menu thoughtfully and then barked their order.

"Hey, Joe," Tony shouted. "Butch would like the spaghetti special, heavy on the meatballs."

Lady was impressed.

In a few minutes, Tony placed a large plate heaping with spaghetti and meatballs before them. It smelled delicious!

Lady took a dainty bite. It tasted as good as it smelled.

As the lovely cocker spaniel was thinking about what an exciting and wonderful evening she was having, Tony and Joe began singing an Italian song about a beautiful night.

This beautiful night, Lady thought, and looked into Tramp's friendly brown eyes.

The Perfect Presents for Eeyore

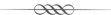

from *Winnie the Pooh and a Day for Eeyore*

ooh was hurrying home after seeing Eeyore. Pooh felt awful. It was Eeyore's birthday, and nobody had remembered to get him a present.

Outside his house he found Piglet. "I have just seen poor Eeyore," he panted, "and he is very sad, because it's his birthday, and nobody has taken any notice of it."

They went inside. Pooh went straight to his cupboard to fetch a small jar of honey.

"I'm giving this to Eeyore as a present. What are *you* going to give?"

Piglet thought for a moment. "I know. I'll give him a balloon. I'll go and get it now!"

So off Piglet trotted, and in the other direction went Pooh.

Pooh hadn't gotten far when a funny feeling began to creep all over him. It was just as if somebody inside him were saying, "Now then, Pooh, time for a little snack."

So he sat down and began to eat from his jar of honey.

Now let me see, he thought, as he took his last lick of honey. Where was I going?

And then, suddenly, he remembered. He had eaten Eeyore's birthday present!

"*Bother!*" said Pooh. "What shall I do?"

For a little while he couldn't think of anything. Then he thought, Well, it's a very nice pot, even if there's no honey in it, and if I washed it clean, and got Owl to write "A Happy Birthday" on it, Eeyore could keep things in it which might be useful.

So, he went to call on Owl.

"Good morning, Owl," he said.

"Good morning, Pooh," said Owl.

"It's Eeyore's birthday," said Pooh. "I'm giving him a useful pot to keep things in, and I wanted to ask you—"

"You ought to write 'A Happy Birthday' on it."

"That's what I wanted to ask you," said Pooh. "Would you write it for me?"

So Owl wrote:

HIPY PAPY BTHUTHDTH THU HDA BTHUTHDY.

"It's nice and long," said Pooh, very much impressed.

"Well, actually," said Owl, "it says 'A Very Happy Birthday with Love from Pooh.'"

"Oh, I see," said Pooh.

In the meantime, Piglet had gone home to get the balloon. He held it very tightly against himself, so that it shouldn't blow away, and he ran to Eeyore as fast as he could. And running along, thinking how pleased Eeyore would be, he didn't look where he was going . . . and fell down flat on his face.

BANG!!!!

It was the balloon.

"Oh, dear!" said Piglet. "Well, it's too late now. I don't have another balloon."

So he trotted on, rather sadly now, and came to the side of the stream where Eeyore was.

"Good morning, Eeyore," he called.

"Good morning, Piglet," said Eeyore.

"Many happy returns of the day," said Piglet.

"Meaning me?" Eeyore turned to stare at Piglet. "My birthday?"

"Of course, Eeyore," Piglet said. "And I've brought you a present. A balloon."

"Balloon?" said Eeyore. "One of those big colored things you blow up?"

"Yes," said Piglet, "but I'm afraid . . . I'm very sorry, Eeyore, but when I was running along to bring it to you, I fell and I burst the balloon."

"My balloon?" said Eeyore at last. "My birthday balloon?"

"Yes, Eeyore," said Piglet. "Here it is. With many happy returns of the day."

"Thank you, Piglet," said Eeyore. "Hmm. It was a red balloon," Eeyore murmured to himself.

Piglet was trying to think of something to say when he heard a shout from the other side of the river. It was Pooh.

"I've brought you a little present," said Pooh excitedly. "Here it is. It's a useful pot. And it's got 'A Very Happy Birthday with Love from Pooh' written on it. And it's for putting things in!"

When Eeyore saw the pot, he became quite excited. "Look, Piglet!" said Eeyore. "I believe my balloon will just go into that pot!"

"I'm very glad," said Pooh happily, "that I thought of giving you a useful pot to put things in."

"I'm very glad," said Piglet happily, "that I thought of giving you something to put in a useful pot."

But Eeyore wasn't listening. He was taking the balloon out, and putting it back again, as happy as could be.

Dawn Patrol

from *The Jungle Book*

s Mowgli shook his panther friend awake, a herd of elephants came into view, marching in single file through the jungle. Their huge feet made a rumbling noise like thunder.

"It's a parade!" Mowgli shouted.

But Bagheera just put his paws over his ears and groaned. "Oh, no—it's Colonel Hathi's Dawn Patrol again!"

"What's the Dawn Patrol?" asked Mowgli. For he was a mancub, and curious as a monkey.

"Every day at dawn," Bagheera explained in a tired voice, "Colonel Hathi drills his herd in military maneuvers. I usually try to be somewhere else at the time."

But Mowgli was fascinated by the grand sight of the elephants marching in formation. And he couldn't resist a parade!

He ran over to get a closer look.

As Mowgli approached the herd, he fell into step beside a baby elephant.

"Hello!" Mowgli cried over the din. "What are you doing?"

"Shhh!" the baby elephant cautioned. "Drilling."

"Can I do it, too?" asked Mowgli.

"Sure," the elephant answered. "Just do what I do. And don't talk in ranks. It's against regulations."

Mowgli got down on all fours and began marching along with the baby elephant. Above the rumble, Colonel Hathi's voice rang loud and clear: "Hup, two, three, four! Keep it up, two, three, four!"

Mowgli was about to ask another question when Colonel Hathi shouted, "Ho! Company, halt!"

The baby elephant turned to Mowgli. "That means stop," he whispered.

Mowgli came to a halt with the rest of the herd.

Colonel Hathi went down the line to inspect his troops.

"Dress up that line!" commanded the Colonel. "Pull in those tails!"

The elephants did as they were told.

Then the Colonel came toward Mowgli.

"Inspection!" the Colonel barked. Instantly, all of the elephants raised their trunks high.

"Psst," the baby elephant whispered to Mowgli. "Quick! Stick your nose up."

Mowgli stuck his nose in the air as high as it would go.

"Like this?" he asked.

"Perfect," said the baby elephant.

Colonel Hathi moved down the line, inspecting each member of his troops.

"Let's have more spit and sparkle on those bayonets!" he shouted at one soldier with dirty tusks. Mowgli stifled a giggle.

Colonel Hathi nodded fondly at the baby elephant, who just so happened to be his son. Then he came to Mowgli.

"Ah, a new recruit," said the Colonel in a satisfied tone.

For one proud and happy moment, Mowgli felt just like one of the herd.

A Royal Pet

Prince Achmed, one of Princess Jasmine's many suitors, stumbled out of the palace. His pride had been wounded, his vanity stung, and the seat of his pants ripped off.

Jasmine thought him the worst suitor of the lot. Ugly. Arrogant. And he had a snakelike, curling mustache that reminded her of her father's cruel adviser, Jafar.

Now she sat by the fountain, thinking. As always, her pet tiger, Rajah, was by her side.

Suddenly Jasmine's sad thoughts were interrupted.

"Jasmine! Jasmine!" It was the Sultan, her father.

Rajah growled right in the Sultan's face, clutching a piece of Prince Achmed's underpants in his teeth.

"So *this* is why Prince Achmed stormed out!" the Sultan cried.

"Oh, Father," Jasmine teased. "Rajah was just playing with him. Weren't you, Rajah?"

"Dearest," the Sultan scolded, "you've got to stop rejecting every suitor who comes to call. The law says you must be married to a prince by your next birthday."

Jasmine sighed. "The law is wrong," she declared, though she knew her father wasn't listening.

She hugged Rajah close. Even if her father didn't understand, Rajah did. He loved her and knew the secrets of her heart. Her pet would do anything to help her. Jasmine realized how lucky she was to have a friend like Rajah.

A Lagoon Tune

from *The Little Mermaid*

It had been such a romantic day for Ariel. Prince Eric had taken her all over his kingdom in his carriage. Ariel loved seeing all the things she had only dreamed of before, living under the sea, but the best part was spending time with Eric.

The only problem was, she couldn't tell him how she felt. Ursula the Sea Witch had taken her voice in payment for changing her into a human being. Ariel longed to know if Eric felt the same way about her, but all she could do was wait and hope that he would say he loved her.

Eric knew he was falling in love with the young woman he had rescued from the beach, but it was so hard to tell how she felt. He
wished there were some way to know what was on her mind.

That evening, Eric took Ariel for a romantic boat ride. Fireflies
glowed all around them. Ariel smiled hopefully at Eric.

"I wish I knew your name," Eric told her.

"Her name is Ariel," whispered Sebastian, Ariel's friend.

"Ariel?" Eric guessed. "That's pretty."

Ariel smiled. Things were going in the right direction.

"So, when's he going to pucker up?" Scuttle the seagull asked
Sebastian. Ariel's friends were getting impatient. They knew that if
Eric didn't fall in love with Ariel by sunset the next day, Ariel would
have to return to Ursula and become her prisoner.

"This boy needs some help," Sebastian decided. He grabbed a reed and held it up like a baton.

The frogs and birds and fish gathered around as Sebastian led them in a romantic love song.

"Go on—kiss the girl," they urged Eric.

Ariel fluttered her eyelashes at Eric. Did he feel the same way about her as she did about him?

The tiny rowboat drifted in the moonlight. It was a magical night. Eric looked at Ariel and knew he was in love with her.

"Kiss the girl!" Sebastian repeated in Eric's ear.

Eric and Ariel leaned toward each other. They were about to kiss when . . .

SPLASH!

Flotsam and Jetsam, Ursula's pet eels, tipped the boat over and dumped Ariel and Eric into the cold water. The moment was ruined.

Ariel sighed as Eric helped her up. Eric had come so close to kissing her! But she knew there would be another chance, because even with no words spoken, she was sure he loved her, too.

Missing: Christopher Robin

from *Pooh's Grand Adventure: The Search for Christopher Robin*

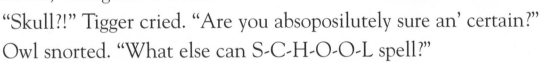

Ever since Winnie the Pooh could remember (which wasn't much further back than yesterday), he could count on meeting Christopher Robin at their favorite place in the Hundred-Acre Wood—a lovely, enchanted hill.

But one day, instead of finding Chrisopher Robin, Pooh found a pot of honey and a note instead.

Later, Owl read the note to Pooh and his friends. "Christopher Robin," Owl declared, "has gone to Skull!"

"Skull?!" Tigger cried. "Are you absoposilutely sure an' certain?"

Owl snorted. "What else can S-C-H-O-O-L spell?"

"You got me there, featherhead," replied Tigger. "Sure sounds terrifryin', don't it?"

Owl and Eeyore and Rabbit and Piglet agreed, and most of all Pooh, who was afraid for his friend. "We must get Christopher Robin back!" Pooh exclaimed.

"Good luck!" said Owl, who had decided not to join the rescue expedition. "Toodle-oo! I'll keep a sharp eye out for your return . . . if you do return, of course."

Owl's farewell made the friends nervous, but not as much as Tigger's talk of the horrible Skullasaurus they were sure to meet at Skull.

Still, the friends trekked on. They picked their way through the Forest of Thorns. They roamed through the Valley of Flowers. They wobbled across the bridge that spanned the Screaming Gorge, and they wandered through the Valley of Mists. After much tramping and tromping, they arrived at Skull Cave.

If they were going to save Christopher Robin, they knew they must venture inside. The friends tiptoed into the deep, dark cave. Inside, something GRRROWLED!

"The Skullasaurus!" cried Piglet. He ran in one direction. Pooh ran in another. Eeyore ran one way. Tigger ran the other.

The friends bumped into one another in the Crystal Cavern. And something found them. It was a shadow. And it GRRROWLED!

The shadow moved toward them. It was Christopher Robin!

"Where have you been?" cried the boy. "I've been searching every-where for you!"

"We've been searching for you!" Piglet cried. "We wanted to save you from Skull!"

"Skull?" said Christopher Robin, smiling. "I was at school."

"But what about the Skullasaurus?" asked Piglet. "We heard him!"

Christopher Robin gently pointed out that the growl was the rumbly tumbly of a hungry-for-honey Pooh Bear.

Then everyone, including Christopher Robin, tramped home for a feast of their favorite foods: haycorn pie for Piglet and Rabbit, thistles for Eeyore, malt extract for Tigger, and honey, of course, for Pooh.

Stories About Courage and Responsibility

Born to Be King

from *The Lion King*

One day, Nala, an old friend of Simba, appeared in the jungle and begged Simba to return to Pride Rock, where Scar, Simba's wicked uncle, had assumed the place of king.

"I can't go back," Simba insisted. "Look, sometimes bad things happen, and there's nothing you can do about it. So why worry?"

Simba told Nala he couldn't help her and walked away.

That night, Simba wandered across a high grassy plain. *What would it prove if I went back to Pride Rock?* he thought. *It won't change anything. You can't change the past.*

As Simba roamed, a baboon jumped out of a tree and followed him. "Will you stop following me?" Simba growled. "Who are you?"

Rafiki said, "The question is: Who are you?"

"I thought I knew." Simba sighed. "But now I'm not so sure."

Rafiki chuckled. "I know who you are. You're Mufasa's boy."

"You knew my father?" Simba asked, amazed.

"Correction!" Rafiki replied. "I *know* your father."

Simba shook his head sadly. "I hate to tell you this, but he died a long time ago."

"Nope!" the baboon chortled. "Wrong again! He's alive. I'll show him to you. You follow old Rafiki. He knows the way!"

Simba followed Rafiki to a pool. Rafiki parted the reeds and said, "Shh. Look down there."

Simba peered into the water, hoping to see a miracle. "That's not my father," he said quietly. "That's just my reflection."

"No," Rafiki insisted. "Look *harder*."

Simba tried. It was true that he looked like Mufasa, but . . .

"See?" said Rafiki. "Your father lives in you."

Then Simba heard Mufasa's regal voice booming from the heavens. He looked up at the stars.

"Simba," commanded Mufasa, "you must take your place in the circle of life. Remember who you are. You are my son, and the one true king. Remember . . . remember . . ."

As the voice faded, Rafiki winked and said, "What was that? The weather . . . very peculiar!"

"Looks like the winds are changing," said Simba.

"Change is good!" replied Rafiki.

"Yeah," said Simba, "but it's not easy. I know what I have to do, but going back means that I'll have to face my past. I've been running from it for so long."

Rafiki lifted his cane and hit Simba on the head.

"Ow!" cried Simba. "What was that for?"

Rafiki laughed. "It doesn't matter. It's in the past!"

"Yeah," said Simba, rubbing his head, "but it still hurts."

"Oh, yes, the past can hurt, but the way I see it, you either run from it . . . or learn from it."

Simba was convinced. He ran through the tall grass, heading for Pride Rock. He *would* challenge Scar. It was time.

Mulan Saves the Day

from *Mulan*

 t the Tung-Shao Pass, high in the snow-covered peaks of
China, the Huns attacked Captain Shang and his troops
without warning. Hundreds of flaming arrows descended
on Shang's men from somewhere up the mountain.

"Get out of range!" Shang cried. "Save the cannons!"

The soldiers carried the cannons back behind some rocks and
aimed them at the enemy.

"Fire!" Shang shouted.

Mulan, disguised as a man, fired a
cannon at the snipers above her.
The rockets exploded,
and the Huns fired back
with more arrows.
Mulan and the other
soldiers ducked.

"Hold the last can-
non!" Shang com-
manded. His troops
waited, peering
through the haze. The
mountains were silent.
As the smoke cleared,
Mulan and the others
gasped. On top of the ridge,
along the entire horizon, stretched a
massive line of Huns. In front rode Shan-Yu, the Hun leader.

In a firm, solemn voice, Shang ordered, "Prepare to fight. If we die,
we die with honor."

"Hee-yah!" cried Shan-Yu, charging down the mountain with his
troops.

"Yao!" Shang shouted to one of his men. "Aim the last cannon at
Shan-Yu!"

Mulan stood beside Yao, her sword drawn. She looked down at her
blade and saw the mountain reflected in its shiny surface. She gazed
up at the mountain, then at the charging Huns.

Quickly Mulan sheathed her sword and grabbed the cannon away from Yao.

"Ping!" called Shang, using the man's name Mulan had invented to disguise herself. "Come back! Ping!"

As Shan-Yu galloped toward her, Mulan carried the cannon up the mountain. Suddenly she stopped. She placed the canon in front of Shan-Yu, then tilted the barrel toward the top of the mountain.

Mulan fired, and the rocket sailed over Shan-Yu's head. It lodged in the overhanging mountaintop, then exploded with a thunderous roar, causing a massive avalanche.

As the wall of snow spilled toward Shan-Yu, the Hun leader glared at Mulan. He had been outwitted! And by an ordinary soldier, no less. Shan-Yu slashed at Mulan, but she hurried away, eager to escape the monstrous force rumbling down the mountain. The avalanche overtook Shan-Yu and his men, and the huns were defeated.

Who's Afraid of the Big Bad Wolf?

from *Three Little Pigs*

nce upon a time, three little pigs lived at the edge of a forest. They were brothers, and their names were Fifer Pig, Fiddler Pig, and Practical Pig. Fifer and Fiddler loved nothing more than to sing and dance all day long. Their brother Practical was more, well, practical. Singing and dancing were fine, he thought, but one must never forget that the big bad wolf lived in the nearby woods.

When it came time for the brothers to build their homes, Fifer and Fiddler were lazy. They quickly threw together rough shacks, one made of straw, the other of sticks. They laughed as they watched their hard-working brother Practical build his own home of sturdy bricks.

"You can't be too careful," Practical warned them. "The wolf may come someday, and then what?"

"Ha!" laughed Fifer and Fiddler. They danced jigs and played music, but Practical went on working until at last his strong house of bricks was finished.

Just as Practical had feared, the wolf soon learned of the fat little pigs living at the edge of the woods. He wasted no time in paying the brothers a visit.

"Little pig, little pig, let me come in!" the wolf barked.

"Not by the hair of my chinny-chin-chin!" squealed Fifer Pig.

"Then I'll huff and I'll puff and I'll blow your house in!" And sure enough, the wolf blew down the house of

straw. Fifer ran to Fiddler's house, and the wolf soon followed.

"Little pigs, little pigs, let me come in!"

"Not by the hairs of our chinny-chin-chins!" squealed the pigs. And so the wolf easily blew down the house of sticks as well.

Quickly the frightened pigs ran to Practical's house.

"Little pigs, little pigs, let me come in!" howled the hungry wolf.

"Not by the hairs of our chinny-chin-chins!" the pigs replied. This time the huffing and puffing did nothing to the solid house of brick.

But the wolf did not give up. The pigs heard him climbing up to the roof. So they lit a fire and boiled some water in a big pot.

Suddenly they heard the wolf slipping down the chimney. He landed with a splash in the pot of boiling water.

"YOWEEEEE!" shrieked the wolf. He leaped back up the chimney as fast as he could and ran back to the forest, never to be seen again.

But just to be on the safe side, Fifer and Fiddler built new brick houses for themselves the very next day.

Dumbo's Fearless Flight

from *Dumbo*

umbo the elephant woke up one morning to the sound of laughter. He blinked his bright blue eyes and rubbed them with the end of his trunk. Something was wrong.

His friend, Timothy Mouse, sat on his shoulder. "Dumbo," he said quietly, "don't look down!"

So Dumbo looked up. In the branches above him perched a flock of crows. They laughed and pointed at Dumbo and Timothy.

"Now I've seen everything!" they chuckled.

Dumbo sat up with a start. He was in a tree! HIGH in a tree! He began to shake with fear. This was even higher than the platform he had to jump from in the circus!

"Hang on, Dumbo!" Timothy shouted. But at that moment, Dumbo slipped and fell with a crash. He felt very embarrassed.

"Hee, hee, hee!" laughed the crows.

Dumbo rubbed his sore head. How in the world did he ever get up in that tree? He couldn't remember much about the night before.

"Hey, maybe you flew up there!" shouted a crow.

"That's it!" Timothy shouted. "Dumbo, you can fly!"

Dumbo wrapped his big ears around himself. Of course he couldn't fly! He could hardly even walk without tripping over his huge ears.

Timothy was sure of it. "Come on, Dumbo, do it again!" he said. One of the crows handed Dumbo a feather. "Here you go, son," the crow said. "You can fly with this magic feather!"

Dumbo carefully held the magic feather in his trunk. Maybe Timothy was right. He closed his eyes, took a deep breath, and jumped from a riverbank.

"You're flying!" shouted Timothy. "Wait till they see this back at the circus!"

It was true. With the magic feather, Dumbo soared through the sky. The crows slapped each other on the back. Imagine, an elephant who could fly!

That night, the big top was packed with people. Everyone wanted to see the flying elephant.

Dumbo smiled at Timothy. With his magic feather tight in his trunk and Timothy tucked in his hat, he stepped off the high platform and spread his big ears. Just then, the feather spun out of his grip. Dumbo was falling!

"Dumbo!" shouted Timothy, "you can fly without the feather! Try! You can do it!"

Dumbo was afraid, but he didn't want to let Timothy down. He closed his eyes tight and concentrated as hard as he could. They had almost fallen to the ground when . . .

SWOOSH! Up in the air Dumbo soared, his ears spread out wide. He and Timothy sailed over the cheering crowd, swooping and diving. Dumbo was a star!

And he didn't need the feather, after all! Dumbo could do it all by himself.

Fit for a Princess

from *Cinderella*

The morning after the ball, Cinderella gazed longingly at the glass slipper, her only reminder of the wonderful time she had spent at the ball. Thanks to her fairy godmother, Cinderella had left her household chores behind and spent one perfect, magical night dancing with a handsome stranger.

When Cinderella heard her stepmother calling, she put the slipper away and hurried downstairs.

As Cinderella stood at the door, she heard her stepmother say to her stepsisters, "The Grand Duke has been hunting all night for the girl who lost her slipper at the ball. The Duke has been ordered to try the glass slipper on every girl in the kingdom, and if the one can be found whose foot fits the slipper, then that girl shall be the Prince's bride!"

Cinderella forgot all about her chores. Last night she had been dancing with the Prince! "I must get dressed," she murmured. "It would never do for the Duke to see me like this. . . ."

Having overheard her, the stepmother knew then that Cinderella had been the girl at the ball. She followed Cinderella upstairs and locked her in her room.

The Grand Duke soon arrived. Anastasia was the first to try on the slipper. "I knew it was my slipper!" she said to the footman. "It's exactly my size." The slipper barely fit over Anastasia's toes. "Oh, well," sputtered Anastasia, "it may be a trifle snug today. You know how it is, dancing all night . . . it's always fit before!"

The Grand Duke sniffed, not believing a word, and asked Drizella to try on the slipper. "Get away from me," she snapped at the footman. "I'll make it fit!"

But nothing Drizella did could make the slipper fit.

As the Grank Duke prepared to leave, Cinderella flew down the stairs. Her friends, the mice, had stolen the key to her room from the stepmother's pocket and freed her.

"May I try on the slipper?" Cinderella cried out. As the footman approached, the stepmother stuck out her cane and tripped him. The glass slipper crashed to the floor and shattered.

The Grand Duke exclaimed, "This is terrible! What will the King say? What will he do?"

Cinderella said, "But perhaps, I can help . . . "

"Nothing can help now," moaned the Grand Duke, his head in his hands.

"But you see," said Cinderella, reaching into her pocket, "I have the other slipper."

The Grand Duke placed the glass slipper on Cinderella's foot. To his delight, it fit perfectly!

And so Cinderella was taken to the palace, where she and the Prince lived happily ever after.

"I Wonder..."

from *Alice in Wonderland*

It had been a curious day for Alice. From the moment she had followed the White Rabbit down his rabbit hole, the most unusual things had happened to her. First she had fallen down through the ground, and now she had landed outside a very tiny door.

Alice peered through the door's keyhole just in time to see the White Rabbit dashing through a garden. He looked at his pocket watch and cried, "I'm late! I'm late!" and was off.

"Oh, Mr. Rabbit!" Alice cried. "Please, wait!" But the White Rabbit was gone.

Alice folded her arms and wondered what she should do next. The door was too small to fit through, and she had no idea where she was.

Just then, Alice spotted a bottle on a table beside her. She picked it up and read the label—DRINK ME.

Alice shrugged. It seemed things couldn't get much worse, so she put the bottle to her lips and gulped.

"Oh! Oh! Oh!" Alice cried in alarm. With each gulp she shrank smaller and smaller. At last she stood in front of the tiny door and saw that she was just the right size to go through it. But when she tried the doorknob, it was locked.

"You need the key," said the doorknob. "It's on the table."

Alice realized that now she was far too small to reach the table. She was getting quite cross with the way things were turning out! Then she saw a small cake with a tag that said EAT ME. So Alice did.

"Oh! Oh! Oh!" Alice cried once again. This time she grew larger and larger with each bite. She could finally reach the key, but now she was too big to fit through the door.

Poor Alice! Nothing was going right! She began to cry. Soon her tears covered the floor and became a river. All sorts of curious creatures swam past as they tried to find a dry spot. Alice quickly drank from the bottle once more, shrank, and climbed inside. The bottle drifted through the keyhole on the river of tears, with Alice inside.

I wonder what Dinah would say if she could see me now, Alice mused, missing her wise cat. There was little time to think of that now, though, for Alice found herself on the other side of the door at last.

Alice got out of the bottle and smoothed her dress. This was certainly turning into an adventure, but she promised herself to be more cautious in the future. There was no going back the way she came, and so she set off through the garden, searching for the White Rabbit and the way back home.

Silly Old Bear

from *Winnie the Pooh and the Honey Tree*

————— ✕✕✕ —————

Pooh was feeling a bit rumbly in his tumbly, as Pooh bears often do.

"Time for a smackerel of something sweet," Pooh decided. Just then, a buzzing honeybee zipped under Pooh's nose. "Aha!" cried Pooh, following the bee. Pooh knew that bees made honey, and wherever the bee went, there was sure to be some. The bee flew into a hive high above Pooh's head.

All Pooh could think about was getting his paws on the honey in that hive. But how? He decided to get Christopher Robin's help.

"Ah, Christopher Robin, I was wondering if you, ah, if you had a balloon?" he asked his friend innocently. "For getting honey, you see."

Christopher Robin gently told Pooh that one doesn't get honey with balloons. However, Pooh had a plan to fool the bees, and the balloon was an important part of it.

Christopher Robin watched as Pooh rolled in some mud until he was covered completely. "What are you supposed to be?" he asked.

"I'm a little black rain cloud, of course," Pooh told him. Then he held tight to the balloon and rose up, up, up to the hive.

Pooh called down to Christopher Robin. "It might help if you picked up your umbrella and said, 'Tut, tut, it looks like rain.'"

"Silly old bear!" Christopher Robin laughed. Pooh's plans never quite worked out the way he hoped. But Christopher Robin did as his friend asked.

The bees were suspicious. They had never seen a rain cloud like this one before! And when Pooh greedily scooped their honey into his mouth, they went into action!

ZOOM! flew the bees, one hundred at a time. Pooh held tight to his balloon as the bees swarmed around him. Buzzzzz, buzzz, buzzz!

Pooh realized that his plan wasn't working. "I think these may be the wrong sort of bees," he said to himself.

The bees kept coming at Pooh. Buzzz, buzzz, buzzz!

"Christopher Robin!" shouted Pooh. "Help!"

The bees crowded around Pooh and his balloon. Suddenly the balloon popped and began to streak through the air. Pooh held on until it was empty. Then he began to fall to the ground with the bees close behind.

"Over here, Pooh!" called Christopher Robin. Christopher Robin and Pooh jumped into the mud puddle as the bees flew past.

"Christopher Robin, you never can tell with bees," mused Pooh.

Jafar's Just Desserts

from *Aladdin*

J afar was determined to destroy Aladdin, Jasmine, and the
Sultan once and for all. With a mighty roar, he unleashed all
his power. The palace crumbled and the earth cracked. Jafar
cackled with evil glee. He knew that even the Genie was no match
for him in strength.

But the Genie had a trick up his sleeve. He had disguised himself
as Aladdin.

"Give it up, Jafar!" the Genie shouted. His stance was bold, though he looked tiny and weak next to the monstrous Jafar. "I'm obviously too much for you to handle!"

"You!" Jafar snarled, enraged beyond rage. His deep voice rumbled and boomed. "You are a fool to challenge me. I am all powerful!"

The Genie taunted him fearlessly in Aladdin's voice. "So all powerful you can't even get rid of a lowly street rat?"

"A problem I mean to rectify right now!" Jafar shouted. Quickly he changed into a huge snake. There was some truth in the Genie's words, but now was his chance to squeeze the life out of Aladdin once and for all!

Jafar grabbed the Genie in one huge red coil. But as Jafar began to squeeze, Aladdin changed right before Jafar's eyes—into the Genie!

"What?!" Jafar gasped.

"Gotcha!" The Genie smiled. He zapped the serpent into a genie—a powerful enemy, but one who would be trapped forever in a magic lamp.

As Jafar disappeared into the lamp, the Genie laughed. "You may be stronger, Jafar, but I've got the brains!"

It's a Good Life!

from *Snow White and the Seven Dwarfs*

Once upon a time, deep in the woods, there lived seven dwarfs: Doc, Dopey, Sleepy, Bashful, Sneezy, Happy, and Grumpy. Their names were all perfectly suited to their personalities.

Since dwarfs are as small as children, their cozy cottage was like a dollhouse. It had a thick wooden door framed by leafy vines. And inside, everything was the perfect size for them.

Despite their different personalities, the dwarfs got along quite well. From sunrise to sunset, they shared the same goal—to do a good job and reap the fruits of their labor.

Every day, after a hearty breakfast of porridge and fresh-baked bread, the Seven Dwarfs would pick up their picks, axes, and shovels and march off to work in the mines.

As they walked, they sang cheerfully. The dwarfs always looked forward to their day. For though their work was hard, it was rewarding.

Dwarfs have an uncanny ability for finding precious metals and stones, and they love fashioning them into beautiful things like necklaces, rings, swords, and crowns.

The dwarfs' jewel mine was in the rocky hills not far from their home, and it was deep and dark. But the dwarfs were used to working underground, and they were not afraid.

Every day, as they swung their picks, chipping away at pieces of rock, they sang a work song. Their low, melodious voices echoed throughout the caverns and tunnels of the mine.

Then, at the end of each day, a clock struck five. One of the dwarfs would look up and cry, "Heigh-ho!"

In a wink, they would all collect their tools and march out of the mine in single file, in the same way as they had come.

Tired yet satisfied, each evening the dwarfs marched down the well-traveled path, whistling and singing. They were content to be heading to their pleasant home after a good day's work, and they always looked forward to the delicious stew that bubbled on the hearth.

Wilbur Takes Wing

from *The Rescuers Down Under*

Bianca and Bernard rushed across the city rooftops, fighting to see through the blinding snow. They finally came to a big birdhouse with a sign that read ALBATROSS AIR.

Bernard peered through the frosty window. "Thank heavens!" he gasped. "The light's on!"

They pushed open the door and dropped their heavy luggage on the floor.

An albatross was dancing around the room, so absorbed in the music that he didn't even notice his tiny customers.

Bianca tapped on his foot. "Excuse us for interrupting," she said. "I'm Miss Bianca, and this is Mr. Bernard. We're from the Rescue Aid Society. We need to charter a flight to Australia."

The albatross bowed and introduced himself. "The name's Wilbur. At your service. Now, when do you want to go? Mid-June would be nice."

"Now," said Bianca. "Tonight."

"What??" squawked Wilbur. "Are you kidding? Have you taken a look outside lately? Sorry, no go."

"But a little boy has been kidnapped," Bernard pleaded. "We need your help."

"K-k-k-kidnapped?" Wilbur sputtered. He was shocked. Then he was angry.

"Nobody's gonna take a little kid's freedom away while I'm around. Okay, storm or no storm, let's go! Just gimme a second to loosen up the ol' back!"

With Bianca and Bernard safely strapped into a sardine tin on Wilbur's back, the albatross took off on a great adventure.

VIKING

Published by the Penguin Group
Penguin Books Ltd, 27 Wrights Lane, London W8 5TZ, England
Penguin Putnam Inc., 375 Hudson Street, New York, New York 10014, USA
Penguin Books Australia Ltd, Ringwood, Victoria, Australia
Penguin Books Canada Ltd, 10 Alcorn Avenue, Toronto, Ontario, Canada M4V 3B2
Penguin Books (NZ) Ltd, Private Bag 102902, NSMC, Auckland, New Zealand

On the World Wide Web at: www.penguin.com

Penguin Books Ltd, Registered Offices: Harmondsworth, Middlesex, England

First published in the USA by Disney Press 1998
Published in Great Britain by Viking 2000
1 3 5 7 9 10 8 6 4 2

Copyright © Disney Enterprises, Inc., 1998

'Wilbur Takes Wing' and 'Bianca and Bernard Down Under' feature characters from the Disney film The Rescuers Down Under suggested by the books by Margery Sharp, The Rescuers and Miss Bianca, published by Little Brown and Company and William Collins Sons and Company
'Dumbo's Fearless Flight' is based on the Walt Disney motion picture Dumbo suggested by the story Dumbo, the Flying Elephant by Helen Aberson and Harold Perl, copyright © Rollabook Publishers, Inc., 1939
'Cruella's Wicked Puppy Plan' is based on The Hundred and One Dalmatians by Dodie Smith, published by Viking Press
'A Forest in Flames' is based on the edition containing the full text of Bambi, A Life in the Woods by Felix Salten, published by Simon & Schuster
'The Trouble with Tiggers', 'Missing: Christopher Robin', 'Silly Old Bear' and 'The Perfect Presents for Eeyore' are all based on Pooh stories by A. A. Milne, copyright © The Pooh Properties Trust
'3-2-1 Blastoff!' and 'Stick Together' are copyright © Disney Enterprises, Inc./Pixar Animation Studios

Made and printed in Italy by De Agostini

All rights reserved. Without limiting the rights under copyright reserved above, no part of this publication may be reproduced, stored in or introduced into a retrieval system, or transmitted, in any form or by any means (electronic, mechanical, photocopying, recording or otherwise), without the prior written permission of both the copyright owner and the above publisher of this book

British Library Cataloguing in Publication Data
A CIP catalogue record for this book is available from the British Library

ISBN 0–670–89402–8